AWAY FROM THE DEAD

AWAY FROM THE DEAD

David Bergen

Edited by Bethany Gibson.
Page design by Erin Russell with Julie Scriver.
Cover image by Thomas Shanahan, iStock.com.
Cover design by Julie Scriver.
Printed in Canada by Friesens.
10 9 8 7 6 5 4 3 2 1

Library and Archives Canada Cataloguing in Publication

Title: Away from the dead / David Bergen.
Names: Bergen, David, 1957- author.
Identifiers: Canadiana (print) 20230140416 | Canadiana (ebook) 20230140424 |
ISBN 9781773103105 (softcover) | ISBN 9781773103112 (EPUB)
Classification: LCC PS8553.E665 A93 2023 | DDC C813/.54—dc23

Also available as an audiobook (ISBN 9781773103532)

The author acknowledges the support of the Canada Council for the Arts, the Manitoba Arts Council, and Winnipeg Arts Council in the writing of this novel.

Goose Lane Editions acknowledges the generous support of the Government of Canada, the Canada Council for the Arts, and the Government of New Brunswick.

Goose Lane Editions is located on the unceded territory of the Wəlastəkwiyik whose ancestors along with the Mi'kmaq and Peskotomuhkati Nations signed Peace and Friendship Treaties with the British Crown in the 1700s.

Goose Lane Editions
500 Beaverbrook Court, Suite 330
Fredericton, New Brunswick
CANADA E3B 5X4
gooselane.com

All this happened without me and I'm writing about it from other people's words.
— Viktor Shklovsky, *Writing Desk*

1.

THE LADY WITH THE DOG

In December 1899 Anton Chekhov published "The Lady with the Dog" in the magazine *Russian Thought*. When Julius Lehn read the story (he made a point of keeping up with what was new in literature), he recognized his student Katka Martens in the main character Anna Sergeyevna — not in her personal circumstances, for Katka was not married like Anna, but in her nature, which was ambivalent and divided, dark and light, torn between rules and passion.

Katka was a university student in Ekaterinoslav who came from Chortitza, a Mennonite colony bordering the Dnieper River. Lehn attempted to seduce her as he had done with other female students. He quoted some poetry backwards. She asked him why he was insulting Pushkin. He lit a cigarette and blew smoke into the corner of the room. She said that he was lazy and self-centred and crude. She had heard, but did not care, that he was popular with the women. He said that he was an atheist, as if to explain his carnal ways. She rolled her eyes and said that faith was more difficult than disbelief. They met once a week in his small room. He made her thick coffee that she did not touch. Even so, he insisted on making it and then, after she refused it, he took it for himself. He learned that both her parents had died when she was five years old and that she had been taken in by her uncle Heinrich and his second wife, Annalee, who raised her as their own daughter. Uncle Heinrich was wealthy and was paying her way through university. She said that she was not sure what she wanted. Her friends were at home and were getting married, and she was here studying languages. For what?

"Do you have someone you plan to marry?" Lehn asked.

"No one."

"Then why worry? Why hunger for something that doesn't exist yet?"

"But it will exist, at least I hope it will, and it can't exist if I don't go home and pursue it."

"Can love only be found at home, in your shtetl?"

"You must stop calling my village a shtetl."

He said that in his experience one could not pursue love. "It falls into your lap, unbidden."

It had been her wish that they meet in his room for tutoring, which was scandalous, and he took it to mean that she was a bit of a libertine. Not true. She simply favoured unpredictability, and she knew that entering his room would provoke gossip, which would allow her to laugh in the faces of those who spread rumours that were not true. She always wore gloves, sometimes linen, sometimes the finest calfskin, because it was cold in his room. She left them on as she took notes and did her exercises. For Lehn it was his fantasy that one day she might remove her gloves, and this would be a signal that she was warming to him. He was twenty-two, she was eighteen. To his mind this

was not such a large gap, to her mind it was an eternity. And
then the fact that he was secular, an atheist. Though he had
been baptized at fifteen, it hadn't been his decision. His father
wanted to escape the Pale of Settlement and had changed his
religion and then the family name from Lehman to Lehn. Her
evaluation was this: he was very good-looking, with his round
gold-rimmed glasses, and the sweetness and light he brought
to each lesson, such enthusiasm for words and sentences and
language, and the careless bravado that hid the inner doubts
that he might not match her, and was less than her, and she
saw this in him, the doubt disguised by certainty, the frail ego
covered up by pretension. The insignificance. He was not yet
full, not yet himself, too much swayed by the surface of things,
like her gloves, which she knew he admired, and knew as well
that he wanted her to remove. And so, she kept them on, and
let him pine.

On a cold afternoon in February 1900, Katka arrived late to her
lesson and entered flustered and apologetic. An old man had
been accosted in the street by two young boys. The boys called
him names and asked for money and the old man fell at some
point and the boys spit on him. No one on the street intervened
and so Katka chased the boys away and helped the man to
stand, and she brushed off his linen jacket and he thanked her,
but she didn't speak Yiddish, and so she didn't understand all
of what he said, though her German helped a little. She felt
pity for him. And she was also angry, that he had not protected
himself better. She wondered if she was gullible and misguided.

Katka sat down and removed her gloves. Held her hands
close to the small fire.

Lehn asked if she didn't want to remove her coat as well. She stood, and he helped her. She was wearing a man's grey button-down shirt with long sleeves — the cuffs fell to the knuckles on her hands — and flannel trousers that she kept pulling up because they were too large for her. She lifted a hand to brush her hair from her eyes. She seemed distracted, she did not really see him. He said that she had a big heart. And then he said that he would like to read her a story.

"Yours?" she asked.

He laughed. "Oh no."

"French?" she asked.

"Russian. A little story by a man called Chekhov." He said that when Chekhov was younger and poorer, he had, just like Lehn, survived by catching and selling goldfinches. "I did that for a time, did I tell you?"

"And so, you are the same," Katka said. She smiled.

"Only in that way," Lehn said. He pulled at an earlobe, which is what he did when nervous. He kept glancing at her hands. He wondered if these hands peeled potatoes and washed the shirt that she wore. There they were.

He sat across from her and read. The story was about a man named Gurov and a woman named Anna who meet while in Yalta. Gurov, who prefers the company of women to men, seduces Anna, who is much younger. Anna, overwhelmed by guilt, weeps. Gurov finds her sentimentality a bother. He eats watermelon and waits for her to finish crying. A fortnight later, after spending every day together, they part. And then meet again in the city of S. And discover that though they are both married, they are in love.

The little story ended this way: "And it seemed as though in a little while the solution would be found, and then a new and splendid life would begin; and it was clear to both of them that they had still a long, long road before them, and that the most complicated and difficult part of it was only just beginning."

When Lehn finished reading, they were both quiet. Finally, Katka spoke. She said that the man in the story, Gurov, was cruel and heartless. "Eating watermelon and dismissing Anna because she feels she has sinned." She called the story amoral. "There is nothing uplifting there."

"But there is. It is love. They are in love. They just don't know how to hold on to that love."

She said that Gurov was too old for Anna. He had used her. And he would continue to use her. All for his own desires.

"What's wrong with desire?" Lehn asked.

"Nothing. If it is equal. And what about the poor wife at home, the 'lower race,' the one who looks twice as old as her husband and calls herself a *thinker*. You like the story because you see yourself in Gurov. And you think I am Anna. You might be him, but I am not her."

Lehn laughed and said that it was true, he preferred the company of women to that of men. He had male friends whom he saw occasionally, but he found their company dull, and he yearned for the voice and face of a woman across from him, but was that because the women were more malleable, more diffident, the "lower race"? Not at all. He loved women because they conversed more intimately, and each interaction was full of play and, yes, if he had to admit it, carried the potential of passion. He spoke about his youth in Odessa. He had worked briefly in the Moldavanka section for a bookbinder, Ariel Folger, whose wife had seduced him, just as Potiphar's wife had seduced Joseph and then denied it. Katka smiled at this, for she of course knew the story of Joseph, and she appreciated Lehn's arcane knowledge, which was a form of wooing — they both felt the frisson of desire, but neither acknowledged it. Lehn said that not all women were beautiful and kind. His own mother had been a harridan, a hard, morose woman who hit him if he came to the supper table with dirty fingernails. "This is why I keep my fingernails short and my hands clean," he said.

◖◗

Katka had left her family on the colony to go to university because she imagined she might escape the strictures of her community. She was stubborn, and wilful, and questioned much of what had been taught her. Lehn was her ticket to another world. A single woman would not go to the tutor's room. She did. She had been raised to wear dresses. She now wore trousers and vests, emulating the women she admired at university, the ones who protested against those in power, the ones who wanted the Tsar removed. It was a thrill for her. She came from money — her uncle Heinrich owned a carriage factory near Chortitza, and he loved her dearly, and when she had become ill at the age of seventeen, it was he who paid for her stay at a sanatorium in Germany. She recovered and came to believe that her mind could defeat the illness in her lungs. She was happy-go-lucky. She saw misfortune as happening to others, not her. She felt that she was too unimportant to die at such a young age. She wasn't in love with Julius Lehn, or maybe she was. She did not know. She waited impatiently for Wednesday afternoons, when she walked over to meet him. Her breathing was quicker than usual, and her heart fluttered, and she was amazed at her foolishness. He had no money. He never spoke of his family, except to say that they had disowned him. He would always be poor.

Their relationship was based on curiosity, and arguments about politics, and desire, and physical proximity: she was seduced by his lack of order, he by her passion.

He talked about the two of them having sex.

She rolled her eyes. And thought that she was always doing this, rolling her eyes, and she should stop. It was unsophisticated, and it was false. She liked it when he was direct.

She said, "None of my cousins, my schoolmates, my relatives, have had sex, unless with a cow. Only when married."

She told him that if anything were to come of this, he would have to meet her family first. She said that that was the first step. She didn't know what the next steps would entail, or if there would even be more steps.

"I am willing to step slowly," he said, though he was suffering impatience and anxiety. He told her that he was like a sculptor working on a very large rock, and he could see the image in the rock, it was completely clear to him, and each knock of the hammer against the marble revealed the smallest progression, but oh, the going was stutteringly slow.

He said that the German language had a fixed order. In a declarative sentence the statement was very certain. *Now we eat.* In Russian the order was more flexible. "It is possible that we will be lovers. And if we aren't today, then we will eat tomorrow." He smiled.

Over the next six months, she became soft towards him and harder towards her upbringing, where she said that wealth had been acquired on the backs of the peasant. She said that her people preached non-violence, they refused to go to war, or to carry guns. "But," she said, "I have seen my uncle take his anger out on his workers. And so, the non-violence is only convenient for avoiding war."

"Avoiding war is good," Lehn said. "I like your people."

She smiled and said that he might find her people too strange. "There are a lot of rules," she said.

"And you are breaking those rules," he said.

She lowered her eyes. Shrugged. She did not want to discuss this further.

One day she arrived for her lesson and accepted the cup of coffee he offered. She added a bit of dark sugar. Stirred it with a spoon. Her hands were shaking. "Now we marry," she said.

He was astounded. He asked if she was doing this to spite her uncle.

She said that that might be true, but there were worse things, weren't there?

He said he loved her.

She said, "So we will marry."

He found an official who could marry them. It would cost, would Katka pay? Yes. They went on a Thursday afternoon. She wore a dress because it was a special day. Lehn borrowed a leather jacket from a friend. And boots that she had ordered for him, because "you can't get married in slippers, or flannel shoes with holes."

The jacket was brown, his trousers were brown, the boots were black.

"Very sad jacket," he said.

She said that the jacket was made from somebody's cow. It was original. She liked it. She reached into a small cloth satchel and folded the money into the official's palm. It was counted. It was sufficient. The official wore the hat of a Cossack. He had been drinking.

"Are you Katka Martens?" the official asked.

"Yes, I am."

"And you are Julius Lehn?"

"Yes."

"Good then," the official said. "You will sign the papers and then be husband and wife."

They signed the papers. One copy for the records, one copy for Lehn and Katka.

"Have a happy life, Mr. and Mrs. Lehn," the official cried out. They left the cavernous building and wandered into the street, holding each other.

"Should we kiss?" Lehn asked.

"Not in public. Wait till we get to your place."

"There is nothing to hide," Lehn said.

"There is everything to wait for," Katka said. She touched his nose with a finger.

They went to his apartment, where he warmed up some soup and cut bread. They ate across from each other. Both were shy.

"How does this work?" Lehn said.

"Let's play first," Katka said. She sat on his lap and stroked the buttons on his shirt. "In addition to this, recite me some Pushkin. Backwards."

He did.

She closed her eyes and listened.

When he was done, she sang a song from her childhood. A hymn. And as she sang, she began to cry.

Lehn touched her jaw and asked what it was. "Is it the soup? The bread?"

"Oh, I am just happy," Katka said. She shivered. Asked him to build up the fire, even though he had little wood left. He stoked the fire. She removed her dress. She was too thin. She apologized. It was her previous illness.

He said no no.

He undressed.

They stood before each other.

"Let me look," she said. And then, after looking for a long while, she said, "Okay, we are ready."

That evening, she lay in bed and watched him rebuild the fire. He too was very thin. She said that she would take him to Chortitza and she would feed him noodles and sausage and cabbage rolls and cream and he would drink milk fresh from the cow.

"My uncle. I worry about him. That he will kill us."

"Is it possible?" Lehn asked.

"Anything is possible," she said.

But they did not go to Chortitza. Instead, she wrote her uncle, to whom she confessed that she had met a young man. He was intelligent, very handsome, educated, and she had married him. Her uncle wrote back, and in the envelope were two letters: one for Katka, one for Lehn.

To Katka he said: I am sorry that we did not celebrate the wedding with you, dear Katka. When you are prepared, bring us the young man so that we might meet. And have a proper wedding. Happiness should be yours. Uncle Heinrich.

To Lehn he wrote: There is justice and there is moderation. There is love of God and the Church. And there is obedience to God, and then to the father. All that I have, the land, the farm, the crops, the horses, the houses, the labourers, all is in my name. It cannot be taken. It cannot be given. It is not yours to have. You are on loan. Don't get proud. Keep your nose to the earth. Katka has suffered illness. You will treat her well. No harm will come to her, financial or physical or spiritual. If there is any misstep, I will beat your head in.

They went to visit the estate six months after they eloped. Katka was worried. She wanted her uncle to like Lehn. He said that if all Mennonites were like her, he had nothing to fear. "They aren't," she said. "And so, you should be fearful." She said that to gain favour with Uncle Heinrich she just had to sing for him. She had once had dreams of becoming an opera singer. She admitted that she had quite the voice. And then she called herself vain. "But it is true, I did have a beautiful voice. Until I became ill." She said that at the sanatorium, when she was seventeen, she had met a young woman her age from Baden-Baden, and she had fallen in love with her. "Our spirits, our hearts, were equal. Before she died, she gave me a picture of her lungs, an X-ray, which I still have."

Uncle Heinrich was waiting on the verandah. He hugged Katka, lifted her off her feet, and said, "My favourite niece."

"Your only niece," Katka cried, and Uncle Heinrich laughed and said that he had been waiting for her to come, and he had been sleeping, and then waiting some more, and then he saw the dust on the road, and he listened for the rattle of the traces, and when the wagon appeared, and she was in it, his soul leaped. "It's been over a year," he said. "How is beautiful Katka?" He took her arm and led her up the wide stairs. He had not acknowledged Lehn, who followed at a distance.

Here was money. Not luxury, for it seemed that the uncle did not believe in luxury, only hard work. Modesty was essential, or the semblance of modesty. Yet pull away that shroud of modesty, and what was revealed was much wealth. Thirty servants. Land. Horses. Livestock. A grand estate. Many rooms in the mansion. Private outhouses. Large clocks built by hand. Manicured yards. A barn grander than any house in town. And better built. Timber frame, post-and-beam. A brickyard, an oil press, stables, orchards neatly manicured.

He would not be sharing a room with Katka. He would sleep with H.H., Martens's son from his first marriage — Martens's first wife, a sister to his present wife, had died of typhus. H.H. was a tall blond man with big hands and feet who spoke Russian with Lehn and looked at him as if inspecting a strange breed of bull. A small bull. Not threatening. H.H. was circumcised. Lehn took a strange comfort in that.

He saw Katka at meals, and even then, they were not seated together. He stared at her longingly across the table, but she appeared to be ignoring him. And then one day, on a Friday afternoon, she hitched two horses to a carriage and told him they were going to visit her uncle Heinrich's factory. Lehn sat on the wooden bench beside Katka and pressed his leg against hers. She wore white gloves. A long dress. A woven straw hat painted white. Her eyes, peering out from beneath the broad rim of the hat, were small grey stones just beneath the surface of clear blue water. She asked him how he liked her family. He said that they were formidable. Especially H.H., who was twice his size. "Yesterday, he captured a hog and held it up in one hand, and tied it to the barn rafter, and cut its throat. The pig squealed and squealed, and H.H. imitated the squeal, and together they were a choir from the underworld."

"Blood frightens you," Katka said.

"I don't like killing."

"But you eat sausage," she said. "And you like your bacon. And your schnitzel."

"You are right. I am a failure."

She leaned into him. Her hat brim scratched his chin. He lifted the brim and kissed her cheek. She allowed this, and so he kissed her again.

"Enough," she said. "This country air is jumbling my mind."

"Have I passed the test so far?" he asked.

"My aunt likes you. Though she says you have a woman's hands."

"If that is my only fault, then I am safe."

"Uncle Heinrich is the final judge. Though I don't need his approval. Just the semblance of it."

He kissed her again. "My heart," he said.

"No, *my* heart. All mine."

Lehn was not inclined to work with his hands, he did not understand machinery, and he had little interest in wood or metalwork, or gears or wheels, other than as a means to move from one point to another. And so, during the tour given by the factory manager, Lehn was more interested in the workers who bent over the bellows and the anvils as they shaped the metal hoops for the wagon wheels and the springs. The heat was immense. The noise made it almost impossible to hear. He smiled at whatever was said, and he nodded. Hoped that he was enthusiastic enough in his responses. He wondered if he would be expected to participate in the family business. And just as quickly, he understood that nothing would be expected of him, except to provide in some way for Katka. He learned quite quickly, through the supper conversations that week, that brute physicality outstripped the life of the mind. Discussions centred on crops and the price of grain and the sale of thirty carriages to a wealthy businessman in Moscow. There was no mention of books or ideas, nor was there curiosity about politics. He sat across from Katka and kept silent.

On the final day of their visit, in the late afternoon, Lehn found himself trapped with Uncle Heinrich in the study. The uncle behind a desk the size of a dining room table, Lehn in a wooden chair that squeaked if he sat back. And so, he leaned forward.

The uncle spoke of his wagons, the best in all of Russia. "Better than the *brischka*, made by the peasants. The wood is oak. The strongest bolts are used. The wheels are iron-rimmed. The suspension is strong, but with enough give so that you can hold a glass of water without spilling. We like to paint the backs of the seats. When Katka was younger, she designed one of the paintings. She is a Christian. Baptized. She follows the Lord. What are you?"

"I was baptized as a ten-year-old."

"Into the Russian church."

"Yes."

"So, you are no longer a Jew."

"I will always be a Jew."

"Of course you will. But do you go to synagogue?"

"I don't."

"I had a synagogue built for my Jewish workers. I am not against the Jews."

"Of course not."

"Why of course not? What does that mean?"

"I can see that you are a fair man. Honest."

"Honest, yes. Fair? You will have to ask my workers."

"Katka loves you."

"And you, do you love her?"

"I do."

"It can't work. Not in my experience."

Lehn did not speak.

"In any case, she has already decided. She is stubborn. And sometimes foolish. What will you do? How will you support her?"

"I do translations. And I teach."

"Is that enough?"

"For now."

Martens waved his hand at the world around him. "You can see all that I have. You understand that it is not yours."

"I don't want it."

"Katka might want it. She is used to this life."

"She has changed."

Martens was quiet. Then he said that there would be a proper wedding.

><

They were married on the estate. Katka wore a white dress with a French bustle. She and Lehn walked in, arm in arm, and sat on garlanded chairs before the minister. The pastor asked them about their love and loyalty, and then he delivered a sermon — Commend thy ways to the Lord — which went on for a good hour, during which Lehn looked down at Katka's hands and then up at her face, which was hidden by the veil. She turned to him once and appeared to smile. When the preacher finally closed his Bible, Katka lifted her veil and showed Lehn her face, and he reached out and touched her cheek and her jaw. There was a string quartet that played during the meal, a mixture of Mennonite and Ukrainian food — potato soup and sausages and buns and cabbage rolls and tarts, and there was wine to drink — but there was no dancing, and Julius was surprised at this, for what is a wedding if one cannot dance. He danced with Katka in the bedroom that night when they were finally and legally alone. He took her hand and said, "Come," and together they danced while Julius sang into her left ear. Katka was afraid to make love in her uncle's house, someone might hear them, and so he ended up talking to her, whispering that he was the luckiest man in the world, and she was the most beautiful woman.

"Do you think so?" she said.

He was not lying.

He was happy to leave the estate. Away from Uncle Heinrich, from the presence of the servants, to whom he spoke as if he were one of them. Away from the young woman who was Katka's maidservant, and who was blind in one eye. It was that blindness that Lehn found disconcerting, as if the proximity of the deformed girl might infect their marriage.

They returned to Ekaterinoslav, to an apartment that had been rented by Uncle Heinrich. Five rooms fully furnished, a view of the park below, and two servants whom Katka promptly dismissed because she didn't want to participate in the subjugation of the worker.

For the first three years of marriage, they were happy. Lehn's desire was purely for Katka, and her desire, though more muted than his, was also directed towards him. Sometimes he wondered if he was too fawning, too unctuous in his affections.

"Do I love you too much?" he asked her.

At first, she laughed and touched his head and said that too much love was impossible. But the question, asked perhaps too often, lodged in her brain, and she began to ask herself the same question. "Does he love me too much?" "Am I simply his vessel?" "Do I have a mind of my own?" "Am I happy?"

He asked her that one morning: "Are you happy?"

"Of course," she said. And she kissed him on the forehead and left for university. She would be gone all day. Lehn taught most mornings, and worked at his translations, and then, after lunch, he slipped into his boots and walked through the city, usually ending up near the university, always surprised by this, but perhaps not so surprised because he knew what he wanted, which was to catch a glimpse of his wife. He wasn't jealous. Or was he? He might have been lonely.

That afternoon, upon returning home, he reread Tolstoy's *Family Happiness* and immediately saw himself as the husband in the story who marries a younger woman. The newlyweds are happy for a time. Two years. And then the young wife, Marya Alexandrovna, becomes bored and restless. She wants to experience others, she wants to be looked at, she wants excitement. And the husband allows this. But he is angry, and confused, and the more confused he becomes, the more he pushes his wife away.

Lehn was more experienced than Katka and had had various lovers, and because of this he had a knowledge of how desire can be slippery, and happiness elusive. Tolstoy wrote, in the voice of Marya: "Now it seemed quite plain and simple; the proper object of life was happiness, and I promised myself much happiness ahead."

But it was impossible — happiness — especially if you promised yourself much happiness or expected that happiness could be willed. True happiness came along with sadness, and sometimes happiness spilled out of a regular life.

To try to explain all this to Katka would have been futile. Her behaviour had changed lately. She had taken up with some of the anarchists at the university, who were followers of Bakunin and Kropotkin. She had become a drinker. She smoked thin cigars. Her language was more vulgar. Sometimes, he imagined disgust in her eyes when she was looking at him.

One evening, she asked him to come to a speech that was to be given at the university. The speaker was a man named Maxim.

"A friend?" Lehn asked.

"An intellectual," she said.

And so he went. And was surprised at Katka's popularity, the men especially who approached her and looked into her eyes and talked to her, ignoring Lehn, who stood off to the side.

When Maxim climbed onto the small stage, Lehn noted that he was very short. He had no neck and a little head. One eye was higher than the other, as if he had spent his thirty years in life squinting at small print in a very small book. At first shy, he began to speak slowly, quietly, and then he picked up speed, or perhaps not speed so much as power, and his high voice lifted, from his wide mouth towards the higher eye, and then talked about ants, and he said that two ants who are from the same nest will approach each other and if one has its crop full, the other will ask for food and it will never refuse and regurgitates a drop of transparent fluid that is licked up by the hungry ant. Regurgitating food for the hungry is a constant recurrence. And if an ant is selfish, and refuses to feed the hungry, the colony will fall upon the selfish ant with greater vehemence than they would upon their enemies.

When Maxim finished speaking, there were cheers from the gathering, and the cheers sounded like many small animals who had gathered strength and were now howling in unison.

Katka was also cheering. Lehn stood quietly beside her. She took his hand and looked at him, all the while opening her mouth, her voice lifting, her eyes angry and full.

They returned home and sat by the stove in their new apartment, the one Uncle Heinrich was paying for. It was late. Lehn said that Maxim's speech was a complete knock-off. Kropotkin's words. Verbatim. "He should have told us that. You don't steal ideas and say that they are your own."

Katka yawned. She didn't want to argue with her husband of three years, who had no political views other than the politics of privacy and solitude.

Lehn pulled at his earlobe and asked, "Are you sleeping with Maxim?"

She laughed and said that everything was to share. Even their bodies. "If Maxim needs feeding, I will feed him."

"So you are the ant with the full crop."

"I will share."

"Do you give him your uncle's money?"

"It is mine to give."

"I am sad," he said.

She said, "Poor Lehn," and she held him.

That night, as she had over the last few weeks, she coughed up blood.

"Is it the chickens?" he asked. "Are you allergic?" She had insisted that they keep a few layers in a cage in one of the extra rooms for fresh eggs, which arrived daily, and when the hen was done laying, she would make good soup. When Katka spoke of chickens and soup, he saw the vestiges of her past, the land and the pigs and the chickens and the grain growing in the vast fields, and he saw that all the money in the world cannot rub the soil from your skin.

Of course, her disease was not from the chickens. It was a sickness that she carried in her lungs. He tried to feed her big meals. She wasn't interested. Go for a walk in the outside air. No desire.

He was ashamed to beg, but he was also aware that he didn't want to have his head beaten in, and so he wrote to Uncle Heinrich. He said: Your niece is very sick. She refuses to seek the help of a doctor. If perhaps you talked to her and told her that she needs the best care, she would find help. She listens to you.

Katka was angry when she learned of the letter.

"You are trying to eliminate me," she cried. "Trying to pull me away from what I love. And it is not Maxim. I don't love him. I admire him."

He listened to her rail, and then listened to her cough and cough, and he carried warm milk to her, and wiped her brow, and fed her soup made from a ham hock.

"Is it poison?" she asked.

Lehn went to a meeting by himself, where he sought out Maxim. He looked down on Maxim's little head and told him that Katka was very ill. That she needed to get help, but she wouldn't, because of her devotion to Maxim. "Can you speak to her?"

Maxim said that he admired Katka. She was a woman with fire in her heart. He loved the fire. He loved her strong heart.

"She is dying," Lehn said.

"I will come," Maxim said.

When he did not come, and did not come, Lehn grew angry and told Katka that Maxim had promised to come, but he hadn't, and what kind of man promises something and then disappears.

"You have no idea of what a visionary is, Julius Lehn. He has a burden to bear, and it is the weight of the poor. He is above others intellectually. How hard that is. How little time there is."

She was sitting in her chair. Her hair was dirty. He said that he would pour her a bath. He boiled water. Mixed the hot and the cold water in the tub, testing it with his wrist, and then helped Katka undress and guided her into the bath. She was too thin. He kneeled by the tub and scooped water up with a bowl and poured the water over her scalp and brow. Some ran down her neck and over her shoulders. Her throat was bare and vulnerable. He thought of the chickens in the cage. He used soap to lather her hair. And when the suds were plentiful, and she was waiting to have her hair rinsed, he said that Uncle Heinrich had sent two train tickets for Badenweiler.

They would leave within a week.

She did not argue.

It was May 1904.

◙

From Ekaterinoslav, up to Kiev, and through Poland into Vienna. Katka passed her days lying in the sleeper, and when she felt slightly stronger, she sat in the observation car, looking out silently at the landscape. In Vienna, she had a burst of energy, and they walked the streets and Katka told Lehn that her uncle Heinrich had taken her to this city to watch an opera, when she was thirteen, and she had told everyone that she would be a singer one day, and she would live here, in Vienna. "And then I became ill. And I stopped singing."

They ate at a small restaurant that held three tables. A

carafe of red wine, which Katka would not touch. Neither did the rack of lamb interest her. Her cheeks were flushed, she was feverish, and in that state she talked quickly and with scattered thinking. She wore a dress. She had in the last while forsaken what Lehn thought of as her revolutionary outfit — trousers, a man's shirt, boots. She began to speak of Maxim. She was sorry.

"But you like me still?" she asked. "Even though I have hurt you?"

Lehn pressed a finger to her lips. "Don't speak of it," he said.

At night, lying in the bunk above her, the carriage swaying, Lehn listened to her breathe, and there were moments when he couldn't hear her, and he climbed from his bed and bent over and put his ear close to her mouth. A small exhalation. A slight intake.

The trip, which should have taken five days, lasted seven. There was a mechanical failure with the engine, and then a delay due to a tree falling across the tracks. Lehn, going out of his mind with worry, climbed from the train to observe the removal of the tree. He was wearing the boots Katka had given him. It was muddy on the embankment and the toes of his boots were now dirty. He bent to scrub at them. In the forward distance, the sound of axes falling, and the shouts of the workers. He thought, When I return to Katka, and if the first word she speaks is my name, then she will live.

An hour later the tree was removed, and Lehn climbed back onto the train. He opened the compartment door. Katka was sitting up. Her face was very pale. She smiled weakly. "Lehn," she said.

In Badenweiler, they stayed at the Villa Fredericke, on the second floor, in a private room. There was a little balcony, with room enough for two, that looked out over a garden below, and in the distance the steeple of a church, and beyond that a tree-lined mountain. It was very quiet — the garden, the nearby streets, the villa. Sometimes, sitting on the verandah, Lehn and Katka heard voices below, a couple speaking Russian. It was not unusual for Russian guests to come and seek the solace of the Black Forest. There was something comforting in having the silence around them broken by a familiar language. One time the couple talked about eggs, and the man said that he was getting used to eating them, they had taken on an improved flavour. He said that he missed coffee. And then the woman said that her tooth ached, and the voices faded. Katka heard none of this. She did not have the concentration to eavesdrop.

In their room there was a small cot, and this is where Lehn slept, and woke to the sound of his wife coughing up blood. And he rose, and washed her face, and held her head, and when she slept again, he sat beside her bed and held her hand. In the morning, around seven, Katka was served acorn cocoa and slabs of butter on dark bread, and around ten they ate porridge together. And then a large meal at one, and another dose of acorn cocoa in the afternoon, and more pats of rich butter, and then the evening meal, which Katka did not touch, as the routine was tiresome. This went on for a month, and then longer. She improved briefly and then suffered a setback.

When she had the energy, they talked about their lives back home. Lehn spoke of children. They would have three. He would take up her uncle's offer of setting up a bookstore in Ekaterinoslav. "Our home will be above the bookstore. We will eat lunch together. You will help with the organizing of the books. We will hire a nanny for the children."

She said that when she was gone, he should remarry. "Someone who is not impetuous. Someone who loves you."

He said again that when she was better, they would have children.

She said that he should count on her uncle. "Here, I will write a note to him, telling him that he is to help with the bookstore." Her hands fluttered and sought out paper and ink. He hushed her.

"It is important," she said. "To my uncle, I am important. He will listen to me. But he can't listen to me when I am dead and gone."

She said, "Your world is too small, Lehn. You see only the covers of books and what is between them. And perhaps a pretty woman in a painting, or on the street, and you think that this is everything. Books and what a woman might offer. Your simplicity will be your downfall. Who will look out for you?"

He shushed her. Held her hand.

That evening he left Katka sleeping, and he slipped out of the villa and walked to a nearby restaurant and ordered soup and bread. The soup was cold, and as he lifted his head to find the waiter to complain, the open shutter on the window was caught in a gust and slammed shut. The waiter hurried over and clasped it, apologizing. It was raining. Lehn felt cold. He forgot about the cold soup. He ordered coffee. He crossed his legs and examined his boots. Surveyed the room. There was a beautiful woman across the room, sitting alone. Lehn drank his coffee and thought about how, in his life before Katka, he would have made it his goal to speak to the beautiful woman, and to perhaps woo her, or at least to discover her name, and if she was married or single, and then to proceed or not, though whether or not the woman was married had never been a deterrent. Katka had cured him of all his little loves.

The following day, July 15, early in the evening, Dr. Schworer appeared and said that he would administer morphine. She was in pain. She had not woken all day. At nine in the evening, she sat up and called for him. He held her hand. "I am here."

"It is funny," she said. "I believed myself invincible. Look at me now." And then she said, "I am so tired."

She closed her eyes. He sat there watching her chest rise and fall, thinking how thin her arms were, and at one point he could not see her breathe, and he panicked and called for the doctor, who arrived and took Katka's pulse. She was still living. She opened her eyes and smiled at Lehn and said, "Are you trying to get rid of me?"

The doctor departed. There was another patient. She fell asleep. He fell asleep. When he woke up, she was dead.

The following day, descending to the main floor of the villa, on his way to send a telegraph to Uncle Heinrich, he came upon a gathering in the main entrance. There was much bustle and porters ran here and there, and in the midst of all this was a young woman who was giving directions. She wore her hair up in a tight bun, her dress was black, and he saw her shoes, which were also black, with laces. More like boots. The woman noticed him and looked away. Stepping out onto the front entrance, he asked the boy in uniform who the woman was.

"Frau Knieper. Chekhov's wife," the boy said.

"He is here? In this place?" Lehn asked.

"No longer," the boy said. He looked down at his feet. "He has left. Gone home. Last night."

"To Russia," Lehn said.

The boy looked startled, and then looked to both sides as if to check for others, and then said, "He passed. Last night."

Lehn turned away. He turned back to the boy, but the boy was gone. He carried on down the street, to the telegraph office, and telegraphed Uncle Heinrich. Katka died. Last night. Much sadness. What should he do with the body? The following day, a wagon drew up outside the villa and two men carried a casket up to Katka's room. They had been hired by Uncle Heinrich. The body would be put on ice and shipped by steamer. Lehn would ride along and keep an eye on the ice. Make sure it was replenished. Lehn marvelled at Heinrich's sway, his imagination. The steamer would depart from Trieste and travel via the Mediterranean and then through the Dardanelles strait and into the Black Sea and then to Odessa and on to Stanislav.

By train they travelled to Trieste. And then boarded the steamer, Lehn above, Katka below. He had very small quarters in which there was a little bed that abutted the wall of the neighbours, an Italian couple on their way to Taganrog. They were rambunctious. He saw them several times during the day, tumbling happily alongside the railing, holding each other. At night, when they made love, he held a blanket over his head, and then, because that did not cover the noise, he accepted his plight and he waited until they were done, but this was brief, and they began all over again. And so, he read. And he sang to himself. And in his head, he wrote letters to his dead wife.

Dear Katka, The heat in my small cabin is over-whelming and so I take walks on the upper deck, where I am not allowed, but no one has stopped me. The German women are poorly dressed, very staid, with no flair. There are a few French women who have taste, and one in particular reminds me of you, in the way she turns her head. It is strange and awful to be talking of other women when you are no longer with me. I am reading Tolstoy's short stories. Was he a happy man? It seems not. Also, Chekhov is dead. There is an Italian couple who sing all night from love. It makes my heart ache. And so forth…

During the stop in Istanbul, he disembarked and searched and searched for ice and then at the last moment found an old man who spoke every language possible, quick with his words, who said in Russian that he had lots of ice, but what was it for? Fish? Oysters? It would cost. They haggled. In the end Lehn paid the old man what he asked and went back to the ship and waited. An hour before the steamer was to depart, the man appeared, leading a cart pulled by a large white dog, water dripping from the cart. The man delivered the ice to the hold where Katka lay in her box, and he watched as Lehn placed the ice around her arms and face and legs. She was dressed in black, with a white lace at her throat, a necklace, her lips blue.

The man did not ask who this was. He seemed to know, for he said that she was very beautiful, and he said that she would be missed. She was too young. He said that long ago he had been married, and his wife had died. She too was young. Like this one. He said that men were like dogs, they needed help in life. Women were stronger than men. He said that he would pray for Lehn. He said again that she was very beautiful. He asked if Lehn had a cigarette. He took one and said it was a good thing the hold of the ship was cold. She would last the trip. He said that Lehn should stay away from the railing of the ship, so as not to fall or even jump into the sea. He would regret it. He said that when his own wife had died, he had not believed her death possible. She had been very beautiful. Like this one. And full of life. Stay away from the railing.

The horn sounded. The old man departed. Back on the lower deck Lehn stood at the railing. The Italian woman appeared and greeted him in Italian. He imitated her. She said something else in Italian, very brief. She had green eyes, she was very short, her ankles were thick, and her hair was long. He said that he did not speak Italian. He said this in her language. She said in French that the cabins were too hot to enjoy. Where was he going? He told her. She asked if he was alone, and he said that he was. She asked if he wanted to take dinner with her and her husband. They had both noticed him and noted him. And then she asked about the ice. She had seen him directing the old man. At this moment the husband appeared. He was not Italian, it turned out, but Turkish. A very large man who took Lehn's small hand and squeezed his fingers like the teats of an udder.

"I invited Mr. Lehn to join us tonight for supper," the woman told her husband.

"Very good." And then he bent to his wife and looked into her green eyes and said something in Turkish. She nodded.

She turned to Lehn and said that her husband was feeling seasick. "He has a weak stomach. Perhaps another night?"

"Of course," Lehn said.

He saw them again that evening, when he appeared in the dining area to take a late drink. They were sitting near the back corner. Mrs. was eating a strawberry torte, Mr. was drinking a liqueur. Mr. seemed no worse for wear. He laughed. He kissed his green-eyed wife's knuckles. He saw Lehn. Acknowledged him and then turned away and poured little adorations into his wife's ears.

In the morning, quite by chance, Lehn took coffee with the Italian woman in the restaurant. She was alone and invited him to join her when he entered. He agreed. They sat across from each other at a table covered in white linen. Silverware. Thin white porcelain cups in thin saucers. He asked the waiter to bring one more setting please. The Italian woman said that he was very thoughtful. She was mistaken. He was thinking of his wife below.

> Dear Katka, I am sitting across from the Italian woman who makes love all night. Her husband is still sleeping. Worn out! She wears her thick hair in a chignon. A dark-blue dress with long sleeves and on each sleeve, at her wrists, six tiny cloth-covered buttons. And grey calfskin gloves! Whereas you were effortless at dressing, even in those old flannel pants that you wore, and your threadbare shirts and leather boots, she appears to work hard at putting herself together. It is quite possible she thinks that I will try to woo her. And then she will take umbrage and reject me. I am gloomy. I am fearfully unhappy. I am most at peace sitting and smoking in the hold at your side. Or standing at the railing looking out over the vast sea, with all its utter indifference to life and death.
> I kiss your little hand.

During a brief stop in Odessa, he disembarked and hired a small cart to take him past his childhood house in the Moldavanka section of the city. The house, in fact more a shack, had disappeared. There was a small sausage factory in its place. He asked the driver to take him by the bookbinder's shop. This was still standing and remained as his nostalgic mind recalled it. It was in this place, after running away from home at the age of seventeen, that he had worked for Ariel Folger. He was given a small cot at the rear of the shop, and he ate leftovers that Folger's wife brought him. He immediately fell in love with the smell of glue and the presses and the starched cloth, and of course with Folger's wife, Ana, who, when she brought him the evening meal, sat with him as he ate. She disliked her husband's false teeth, which he removed too often and too soon in the evening. He was old. She was young. She wore grey leather high heels that accented her calves. A red skirt. Bishop-sleeve stand-collar chiffon blouses. She took Lehn's hands in hers and asked him to recite some poetry. To impress her, he quoted Pushkin backwards. His affair with Ana Folger ended when he asked her to run away with him. "But to where?" she asked. "And how? With what?" And she laughed. Even so, he loved her mouth when she laughed. And her pink tongue, which accused him of seducing her one evening when she was caught in his room by Folger, her hair loose, her high boots at the foot of the bed. And so, he was thrown out.

Now, sitting in the low-slung cart, he questioned his desire for nostalgia. And at the same time wondered if Ana, his older lover, would appear. What was he looking for?

Dear Katka, I am lost…

He called out to the young boy to ride on. It was more than five years since he had left this place. He wondered about his brothers and sisters. Briefly. And then forgot them. His heart was cold and indifferent. What had he expected? A reunion with a past that he detested?

The steamer travelled on from Odessa to Stanislav, where Lehn replenished the ice and boarded a boat that was going up the Dnieper River. By the time he arrived at Chortitza, poor Katka was physically depleted. Her face was flattened by gravity, and the melting ice had created a bath of sorts, and the whole affair had turned unseemly. She couldn't be buried soon enough. And so it was that Uncle Heinrich arranged for the funeral to take place the following day. It was a large funeral, sombre and dark, with much lamenting and singing that was dirge-like but sometimes rose to heights of tremendous power, the voices of the people rising and rising so that Lehn was carried away. He had not heard voices or singing like this before, and he wished now that he had gone to church with Katka and heard her sing with her people.

2.

Heartache Comes Crawling Up from the Floors

Katka had written to her uncle before she died, and in her letter she asked for financial aid for her husband. She concluded, As you know, being who he is, he cannot buy his own bookshop, and so you will have to put it in your name. Lehn is a good man. He is my love. Trust me. You will not be disappointed.

Lehn read the letter on the boat trip up the Dnieper, and then resealed it. Considered, out of pride, burning it. Never, during their marriage, had Katka referred to him in that way — *who he is*. And now, reading her description, he was aware that this is how she had seen him. It was not how he saw himself. He was an intellectual, a translator, a sophisticated man who happened to have been born to a Jewish mother and father in Odessa. He did not care for religion, or ethnicity. If someone had asked him if he was Jewish, he would have said that he was Russian. Or he was Ukrainian. To identify as Jewish was to say he was a certain bird with blue feathers. The blue feathers were inconsequential to him, though he knew

that the colour of his feathers meant a lot to others. That he was
a bird, like all other birds, was the most important thing. He
delivered the letter to Martens, who suggested that Lehn might
want to work in the carriage factory. Lehn said that his hands
were clumsy, not made for factory work. And so, Katka's uncle
bought a small shop in Ekaterinoslav where Lehn sold books.
It was agreed that 20 per cent of all sales would go to Martens.

Lehn moved out of the furnished apartment with five rooms
that he had shared with Katka and settled into the apartment
above the bookshop where there was a small wood stove, and
a bed, and shelves for dishes and clothes. In that first while, he
took to sleeping with one of Katka's shirts that still held her
smell. He laid it across his pillow. Eventually the shirt lost all
scent of her, and he folded it and placed it on one of the shelves
in the small room and sought out another piece of her clothing.
He discovered that her intimate wear, the clothing that had
touched her skin, was more likely to still hold her smell. And
so he slept with her camisole, her stockings, her underwear.

Sometimes, on weekends, he travelled back to the colony,
to Rosental, where there was a small house that Martens had
provided for Katka and him, in the hopes that the two of them
would settle down and have a family and live out their days
in a domestic manner with Katka's people. But Katka had
preferred city life and so the house was rented to one landless
family, and another, and then it was empty, and Lehn began
to make use of it on those odd Saturdays and Sundays. He was
viewed circumspectly by his neighbours, who first called him
Widower Lehn and then, when there was no new marriage,
Lonely Lehn. Lehn understood that being given a label was a
form of affection. He spoke some Low German — like Yiddish,
it was guttural and base and descriptive — but not enough to

communicate well, and so he used Ukrainian and Russian, and occasionally a mix of High and Low German. When he did appear on the weekends, his neighbour to the south, Mrs. Peta Goerzen, would deliver fresh buns and bread to him and ask if he was going to church the next day. He said no. She said that God knew his sorrow — this was a year after Katka had died. She said, "Are not two sparrows sold for a kopek? And one of them shall not fall on the ground without your Father's consent." She was greatly pregnant, her cheeks were fat and healthy, and as she walked, she moved like a wagon full of hay, swaying slightly, richly laden. She laid down her offering of buns and backed from Lehn's house. She called out that the buns should be eaten while still warm. With butter. And watermelon syrup.

The village, in general, felt sorry for Lehn, and he sensed this. When Corner Koop died suddenly, Mrs. Goerzen hinted that Lehn might be interested in the widow, Tina. She was twenty-two, and strong, with wide hips. There were only two children so far. Goerzen said Tina was a reader of Russian novels. When Lehn talked with Tina, two months after the funeral, he discovered that it was her husband who had liked Russian novels. And so Lehn bought the meagre library from Tina and carried the books to Ekaterinoslav. It turned out that there was a Russian translation of *Adventures of Huckleberry Finn*, and when Lehn read it, he deemed it worthwhile, but not as funny as he had imagined. There were a lot of coincidences in the novel.

He hired a woman to help with the shop in Ekaterinoslav. Her name was Irena. She was single, a former university student with very decided ideas, like Katka, only she was not Katka. Irena slept in the apartment above the shop, and when

Lehn was in Ekaterinoslav, he shared the space with her. He believed that she might have other men. There was sometimes evidence of a male presence in the apartment when he arrived on Monday morning. A cigarette in an ashtray. A pair of socks too large for Irena. He did not ask. He did not want to be controlled, and therefore he would not control others. Irena was very efficient with money. And she was organized. And so, his business flourished.

One Monday evening, after the shop was shuttered and he had eaten cold sausage and bread with Irena, they were sitting in chairs, their knees touching. Lehn told her the story of Katka's death. That afternoon he had sold a rare Chekhov book to a prince from Saratov, who was in Ekaterinoslav on business. The prince was a collector, among other things, and he had spent a good hour in the bookshop, flipping through *The Kingdom of God* by Tolstoy and then dismissing it as the utterings of a sentimental man gone mad. "He was such a fine writer, full of clarity, and then he fell in love with poverty," the prince said. "Or those who were poor. The peasant." He asked Lehn if he had any Chekhov. He was always on the lookout for the early work.

Lehn had a first printing of *Dyadya Vanya*. He showed it to the prince, who put on gloves to hold it. "Of course, I will take it," he said.

"But you don't know the price," Lehn said.

"I will pay what you ask. It is priceless."

Lehn suggested an exorbitant price, hoping the prince would refuse.

"Sold," said the prince. "We will make arrangements."

And then the prince said he had always wanted to meet the playwright, in fact there had been an occasion when he had heard that Chekhov was to be at a certain dinner the prince himself would be attending, but the evening came and went and there was no sign of the great man. "Perhaps he was already ill," the prince said.

He said that he wanted the book delivered to his estate in Saratov. A long distance, but he would pay the charges. He gave his name: Prince V.V. Saburov. He looked forward to the book arriving safely.

There had been no mention of when or how Lehn would be paid. Lehn had simply agreed, shaken the prince's hand, and wished him a safe voyage.

Alone once again, Lehn lit a cigarette in the backroom. He would not send *Dyadya Vanya* to the prince. He loved it too much. This was one of his problems, being unable to let go of what he loved, especially a certain book.

In the evening, sitting knee to knee across from Irena, Lehn told her about Saburov. And the book. And the prince's wish to meet Chekhov.

Irena said that rich men were always looking for ways to touch the shirt sleeves of the intellectual and the famous. Money didn't seem to be enough. Though Chekhov was an exception. He was amoral.

"I don't think so," Lehn said. And then, as if it couldn't be otherwise, he told her of the sanatorium in the Black Forest, and of his wife Katka, and her death. And of Chekhov, who was dying in the room beneath them.

"You knew it was Anton Chekhov below you?" Irena asked.

"It was. I was told the following morning that he had died at the inn where we were. On July 15, 1904."

"But you never met."

"He died before I could meet him."

Irena laughed. "It's a good story."

"You don't believe me."

"Absolutely. I just don't trust stories. That is why we call them stories. They are made up for a greater purpose, not because they are true."

"This happened."

"Of course, of course. But what is the purpose in the story? Next you will tell me that you and Gorky are best friends, which again has little purpose other than gossip."

"I have never met Gorky." He felt shame. He had betrayed Katka by revealing the manner of her death, but more than that, he had made Chekhov the central character in his story, and it should have been Katka whom he extolled and developed. Why had he done this? To impress Irena? He was no better than those who, as Irena said, wanted to brush shoulders with the famous.

He felt ill. He took it out on Irena. Later that evening he and Irena ate eggs and drank tea in the apartment. She had a long face, her hands were reddened and veined, perhaps from being cold all the time, for she never wore gloves.

"Your hands are chapped," he said. "Do you need gloves?"

She dropped her hands to her lap and hid them.

They were quiet the rest of the meal. The next day, in the shop, she was wearing calfskin gloves that must have cost a fortune. He felt bad for his behaviour, but he was also pleased. He kissed her and called her beautiful.

"You are so simple, Julius," she said, and kissed him back.

And now, when they made love, she asked him if he wanted her gloves on or off, and he sometimes said on and sometimes off, and when it was off, he removed them for her.

◧

During the revolution of 1905 Lehn turned into a beetle scuttling about, bowing his head. On the street he hid, for there were ruffians at large, looking for targets, and because he had blue feathers, he was a good target. And so, he avoided the squares, and the public areas, and he did not go out after dark. He started doing push-ups, in the back of his shop, in order to fill himself out, in order to not look weak. Irena laughed and said that he should do push-ups on top of her, come, now, and his throat became husky, and he could not speak save for a whisper and this was how Irena knew that he wanted her. She locked the door and dragged him up to the small room above the bookshop and undressed herself and then him and had him do push-ups naked above her, and so on. He did not mind. In the moment. Only later did he feel wretched and humiliated by how he had allowed her to control and punch at him. And yet he had called out for more. He was always sore after, with bruises on his chest and arms. He lacked self-control.

News came that his brother had been killed in Odessa. Hanged. His brother had a small shop, a garden out of which he sold flowers and plants and trees. What harm in that? Seven children, it turned out, who were now fatherless.

The Tsar would fall, it was certain, and there were celebrations in the street. Irena said that it was about time. And then she began to spend time with a young university student she had found at a rally. Lehn had met the young man, quite unattractive, with a small chin and long hair, who posed as a worker. The young man's name was Yuri, and he hated men like Lehn. It was easy to know this. Once you have experienced it, you know the smell of it, the eyes squeezed shut, assessing. The nose lifting above the sneer. Yuri took one of his most precious books, the first edition Isakov Pushkin — a binding of school-boy calico, in a brownish black — and when Lehn discovered this, he confronted Irena.

"You're too in love with things," Irena said.

"Books are not shoes. If we equate them, then we simply become materialists. Where has the soul gone?"

"Dear sweet Lehn. You must be careful. You are naive."

"Don't bring him around here." He was standing over her, spitting his words onto the top of her head.

She had cut her hair short, and her large ears showed. She shrugged. And left him standing there. He was not a violent man.

The next day, she was gone. And now Lehn was lonely. And now had to do his own shopping in the market. And now buy his own cigarettes. And now wash his pants and shirts and socks. And now sleep alone. He closed the shop for two weeks and made his way back to his house in Rosental, where the villagers were surprised to see him. What about his shop? His work? His life? When would he marry?

But the Tsar did not fall. Within that year he teetered, and returned, and with his return, and the beginning of the Duma, the world turned back into a semblance of its former shape, and retribution was meted out by the wealthy, who had been attacked by the peasants. So now landowners hanged and shot the workers who had dared to revolt. Revenge was in the air, and the smell was foul. Lehn had no interest in pursuing those who had pursued him. Let me read, he thought. Let me sell my books. Leave me alone.

One Sunday he went to the Martens estate for *faspa*. The two sons, Wenig and Arden, nine and eight, sat on either side of Mr. Martens. They were polite at the table, with impeccable manners, though Lehn saw them later out behind the stable, throwing a cat against the wall. The boys did not see him, but he turned away, full of shame for the boys, and himself. Strange that he should feel shame for himself.

H.H. was there as well, still living with his father and step-mother. He was now in his twenties, still sullen, and he still paid scarce attention to Lehn. He told the story of hanging two rebel peasants the week before. It was his duty as a land captain to maintain order.

Martens was quiet as H.H. talked and talked about retribution, about land rules, about the dangers of acquiescence. And then, as H.H. was mid-sentence, Martens said, "Enough."

That was that. But Lehn was shaken. He looked at H.H.'s hands. They were soft and untrammelled. Did they know how to make a noose?

Mrs. Martens offered rice pudding.

The younger boys were dismissed.

Lehn studied his plate, his hands on his knees, as H.H. talked about order.

"The job has gotten to your head," Martens said. "It is ours to forgive. It is God's to wreak justice."

"In that manner, you and all the pacifist landowners will lose everything."

"The Lord giveth and the Lord taketh," Martens said.

Mr. Martens turned to Lehn. He wanted to know about the bookshop. Was it successful?

"Very," Lehn said. He said that the previous month he had purchased the complete library of an estate owner who had died suddenly. The family, in their haste and grief, had asked him to take the collection off their hands for a certain sum. Only later, Lehn said, in going through the books, had he realized that the collection had many originals and first editions. An original of *The House of the Dead*, for example. Mr. Martens lifted his head and waited, as if there might be more to this story. H.H. grunted.

"By Dostoevsky," Lehn said.

"A reprobate," H.H. said.

Lehn pulled at his earlobe, and then turned to Martens and told him about the prince who had come looking for rare books and had found *Dyadya Vanya*. When Lehn told Martens the price offered, Martens sucked air between his teeth.

"God in heaven," Martens said. "That kind of money for a made-up story?" He turned to his wife and said, "I should give up on wagons and begin to write books." He looked at Lehn and winked.

"When will you remarry?" Martens asked. "Have children. Settle down."

"It is too soon," Lehn said.

Mrs. Martens said that on a practical level it was necessary to find a new wife. "Katka would have wanted this. A man needs a wife."

"Perhaps our Lehn already has someone in mind," H.H. said. "Or he keeps one secretly."

"No secrets," Lehn said.

"Every man has secrets," H.H. said. He rolled a cigarette, his large hands very nimble, and said, "What did our Lehn think of the uprisings?"

Lehn knew there was a correct answer. Still, he said, "'Our Lehn' thinks it is worse for some than for others."

Mrs. Martens looked at him quickly and then looked over at H.H., who was now holding his rolled cigarette, unlit, between his fingers.

Was the man dangerous?

"It was chaos," Lehn said, which was the correct word for his audience, and a safer answer.

"There will be more chaos. Perhaps even a civil war," H.H. said. He stood and stretched. A big man. He went to Mrs. Martens and kissed her head and thanked her for the meal. He left.

Mrs. Martens also excused herself. Lehn noted that she was still very young, and that she hid her beauty behind undecorated dresses and a severe hairstyle.

"Ignore H.H.," Martens said. "He is impetuous, and stubborn, and full of wrong ideas. But I love him. This is what happens. Our boys become men, and then they are beyond our control. And we hope that we have raised them correctly. His mother died too young, and so he had a nursemaid, and then a nanny, and then others, and each was not good enough, or perhaps H.H. was too difficult. Blood is thick, though. This is why you must find someone and have children."

A young girl entered to pour coffee and clear the plates. Mr. Martens spoke Ukrainian with her. He called her by her first name, Nastja. He thanked her. She blushed and scurried away. Her elbows were bare, and sharp, her teeth were big. He would notice Nastja later, in the yard on the side of the manor by the wooden pickets, H.H. talking to her, a hand on her, her head bowed, and it seemed intimate, the encounter, or perhaps it was dangerous. The girl's small head, her sharp chin, big teeth.

This was the sort of thing Lehn noticed. Like he noticed Mr. Martens's beard, and his lack of moustache, which made his head bottom-heavy, and gave the illusion of a man being pulled earthward. Though, when he spoke, his voice was high-pitched and so he was once again lifted towards heaven. He spoke now. He wanted to know the numbers from the bookshop. He had made his investment and needed to have proof of success. Or failure. Lehn, as he laid out the numbers, proved that he was successful, so far — though, with the unrest, who knew.

"No one knows," Mr. Martens said. "Only God in heaven."

◤◢

At first, after Katka's death, there were mornings when he woke from a dream in which he was feeding Katka bits of bread, and sips of soup, and she was smiling at him, and then upon opening his eyes he found himself alone, and without comfort, and if he had been a man who wept, he would have. He lost himself in women, and in drink, and in books. The women were temporary, the drink was essential, and the books were irreplaceable. Two years had passed since her death. It seemed an eternity. And yet, if asked, Lehn would have said that Katka had just died yesterday. And so, time was a paradox. He was a moving body on a swiftly moving train, and he was hurtling towards his own death. Outside the train, in the field, he saw Katka appear and then just as quickly disappear. He was moving too quickly, and only in his dreams could he achieve her physical presence. Here you are, he said, and then he woke.

Another year, and then another, and another. Irena had been replaced by Olga, who was replaced by Zenya, who was taken over by Natalia, and then Karine, and each of them was indistinguishable simply because they all exuded pity for him.

He approached them as if seeking a solid comfort, ears that were attuned to him, eyes that followed him, until something went sour or amiss, and the eyes and ears became unattractive, or a nuisance, or he disliked what this or that woman might see in him — someone of little consequence — and what was a cruelty towards himself turned into a cruelty towards his various lovers. It was not pretty. All it took sometimes was the sight of the bunion on his lover's left foot, very much like his own bunion, but why should she be flawed? How could he love a woman with a bunion on her left foot?

Katka's death had made him aware of his mortality. Still, death did not frighten him, for he knew that once he was dead, he was dead. He would no longer be conscious of people touching his corpse, studying him, burying him. Just as Katka had been an object that he had covered in ice. To what end? To preserve her, to keep her whole? Impossible. The ignominy of those days on the ship made him sad and angry. How awful she had looked in the casket at the funeral. But perhaps he *was* afraid of death. And that is why he could not live alone and had to find another woman as soon as the last one had deserted him. Abandonment terrified him. Sex was important. It was the only way he could verify his existence. Even books, for a time, had lost their capacity to comfort him. Touching the flesh of a woman was the only thing that kept him from shooting himself in the head. Though he didn't have a gun. And, ultimately, he didn't want to die.

◄►

When Lev Tolstoy died, he wept. Karine, with whom he shared the room upstairs, was astounded at the emotion he exhibited. He picked up *War and Peace* and opened it at random to the scene where Natasha is about to be kidnapped by Anatole Kuragin. Listen, he said to Karine, and he read her several pages, his throat husky with emotion, and finally tears rolled down his face. "It carries you away," he said. "So much emotion, but Tolstoy doesn't overdo it, he just tells the story, and we feel everything. We want Anatole dead, we want Natasha to fall in love with Pierre." Karine touched his hand and said that deep down he was a sentimental man, and this was an attractive trait. Though what did he feel for the beggar on the street? Did he love the beggar as much as Lev Tolstoy?

What a question. And insulting to the great writer to equate him with a beggar. "There are gods, and there are mortals," Lehn said. "Tolstoy was a god."

Of the things that Lehn did not know about himself — and there were many aspects of his life that were hidden from him — was the fact that he measured the timeline of his own life by the lives of the writers he admired, and by their influence upon him, and by the confluence of their words and his actions. And so, Pushkin looked down upon his youthful affair with the cobbler's wife. And Katka's love for him began when they sat together in his cold apartment and he read her "The Lady with the Dog." And Katka's death was overwhelmed by the death of Chekhov — not that he loved Chekhov more than Katka, not at all, but that fate should bring their lives together for one moment, and that he, Julius Lehn, should be left to live when Chekhov and Katka were dead, that fact alone amazed him. It only augmented his insignificance and his shame, that he should talk about Chekhov's death in Germany but say nothing about his dear Katka. Which was why he took such umbrage when Irena had told the story to regular customers. It was disgraceful. And now the death of Tolstoy. Many years later he would recall a woman touching his hand and calling him sentimental, but he would not remember her face, or the sound of her voice, for the moment was about Tolstoy, and he would recall the pages that he read to the woman across from him — he knew the exact page numbers — and how significant the words were, and how beautiful, which made him feel beautiful himself, for isn't that what great stories did, elevate the reader?

Years later, while civil war raged through Russia, Maxim Gorky would publish his recollections of Lev Tolstoy. And Lehn would find an early copy, and hoard it, of course, and would not sell it, but read it several times, and memorize certain passages, such as this one, where Tolstoy says,

> *Once a person has learned to think, whatever else he may be thinking about, he is also thinking about his own death. You can see it in all the philosophers. And what kind of truths can there be if death is on the way?*

What kind of truths indeed? The world stank.

◄◙►

The sun, the moon, the seasons, and the years, all came and went, and up until 1915, when Russia had entered yet another war, Lehn spent his time travelling to various estates where a library was for sale, or he might have heard of a rare book that was available, and he travelled by train to find that book, in one case it was a first edition of *The Idiot*, and though he found Dostoevsky bombastic and nationalistic — so much talk about the Russian soul — he knew that a book collector might one day appear and pay a good sum for that particular edition of *The Idiot*. For Lehn, the war was outside noise, events that were happening elsewhere, though he would certainly be affected. In that year, Gorky visited Ekaterinoslav. Or this was the rumour. Karine, who was still with Lehn — he continued to be astonished by her fealty to him and to his shop — told him that she had heard this from another bookseller. Gorky was very famous. Photographs of him were everywhere, on postcards, matchboxes, cigarette packs. He was handsome, with thick dark hair. Lehn envied the hair. There was a photo in which Gorky was wearing a fedora and a wool coat with a wide collar, his left hand on his hip, eyes looking straight, and when Lehn showed it to Karine, she said that here was a man who knew himself. "Look at him! A working man." Which was the impression he wanted to give, Lehn believed.

In the unlikely chance that Gorky might visit the book-shop, Karine placed all of Gorky's books in the shop window, carefully displayed, with the angles just so. She dusted the shelves, dressed herself up, told Lehn to prepare. Lehn was doubtful that the man was even in the city, but Karine's belief was infectious, and he found himself waiting, looking up every time someone entered the shop, and experiencing a slight slope in his emotions when the person who entered turned out not to be Gorky. He was foolish, but he enjoyed the foolishness, the wait.

He did not come. Of course not. It turned out that the rumour had been exactly that, a rumour. The writer had never visited Ekaterinoslav. But the books remained in the window, and Karine kept dusting them. And the war picked up speed. The streets were full of soldiers.

That autumn, just after the Gorky incident, Lehn was invited to attend the wedding of Martens's son Wenig, to take place on the estate. A cousin was to fly in on his own plane from Moscow. There would be gratitude for God's gifts. The celebration of love. Lehn was cynical about love, but he could not refuse his benefactor, Heinrich Martens. And so he went, wearing the same suit and tie that he had worn on the steamer from Trieste to Turkey, ten years earlier. It was still in good enough shape. He was the same weight. It fit. And it was at the wedding that a young woman caught his eye. He tried to turn away, but she kept appearing, enthusiastic and naive. He was thirty-seven. She was seventeen. How old was Pierre and how young was Natasha in *War and Peace*? Did they not find love? Anything was possible.

3.

POOR FOLK

Sablin and Inna were the son and daughter of a landless family that lived in a toiler's hut at the edge of the Martens estate. Their father, a peasant whose family came from a nearby Ukrainian village, cared for the horses in the stables of the estate. Then he was gone, down to Crimea, soon he would send for them. He was not heard from again. The mother, a Mennonite who straddled two worlds, worked in the estate kitchen, baking bread, scrubbing pots. When the children were young, they trailed after their mother and kept hidden while she worked. One day, the estate owner's wife, Annalee, discovered Inna. She scooped her up and took her away for the day, and when she brought her back, Inna was wearing a new dress. And so it happened that Annalee became very fond of Inna. She treated her as her own daughter, or perhaps she was a replacement for her niece Katka. She fed Inna richly. She insisted that the girl go to school. Sablin, on the other hand, was kept hidden. With his mouse-coloured hair, and his small head, he blended in with the peasants. Eventually, Sablin's mother arranged for him to work in the stables of the estate, and in the evenings the three of them walked back to their hut, Inna in her fine clothes, carrying her pencils and her notebook, Sablin holding his mother's hand, talking about the horses. They ate late, usually soup, and sometimes with the soup a half loaf of bread that their mother had taken from the kitchen, hidden under her dress.

In the fall of 1914, when Sablin was seventeen and Inna sixteen, they went with their mother to the estate for a hog roast. Sablin wore clothes his father had abandoned, polished boots and black pants with black braces, a button-down shirt that was pale from much washing. The women wore dresses. Inna wore boots given to her by Mrs. Martens. Wax aglets. Lace hooks. Her legs were bare. It was a Saturday, in late fall. The point of the gathering was for Martens to be praised for his generosity. The workers were all present. Stable hands, millers, mechanics, carpenters, maids, cooks. Children flew about. Martens's wife, Annalee, was there, along with their two sons, Arden and Little Heinrich — named after his father — and to delineate who was who, he was called the diminutive, Wenig. The sons were slightly older than Sablin and Inna. They saw themselves as superior to the workers and the peasants. They wore flower water and oil in their hair. Wenig had a moustache. He had been baptized last year. Neither of them spoke to the workers, though Wenig rode his horse in amongst the peasants as they sat on bales and ate pork and buns. He was tolerated. He flirted briefly with the young Mennonite women who worked on the estate, and then he spied Inna. He approached, dismounted, and asked her name. She gave it. Sablin, who sat beside her, was aware of Wenig's wide mouth and his sparse moustache. Wenig said that he had not seen Inna before. Why was that?

"I have been here," Inna said. "You've seen me. I've shared your table."

"You've grown, then. Your legs are strong," Wenig said.

Inna bowed her head.

Sablin looked off into the distance, where the children ran. His ears were ringing.

Wenig asked Inna if she could ride.

"Horse?" she asked.

"What else, a donkey?"

"We don't have a horse," Inna said. "Though my brother rides. He knows horses."

"Is that right?" Wenig looked at Sablin. Then back at Inna. He asked where her brother learned to ride.

"From my father. He worked in the stables here. For your father."

"And now?" Wenig asked.

"He's gone."

"Is he dead?"

Inna shook her head. "Travelling," she said.

Wenig tilted his head. Gathered up the reins and mounted. He looked down at the brother and sister.

"Is your brother mute?" he asked.

"He can talk. He just doesn't want to."

"Huh. Well. Eat up. Enjoy the food." And then he said her name, Inna, and he nodded his head and kicked at his horse and wound his way out to the large expanse of grass.

Inna giggled.

"What are you laughing at?" Sablin said.

"Mute," Inna said, and she giggled again.

"Stay away from him," Sablin said. "He's greedy."

"Not going near him," Inna said.

Later, in the falling light, the workers played a game with sticks and a ball. They broke up into haphazard teams and played until darkness came. Wenig watched from his horse, riding back and forth. The mosquitoes came and the women danced and swatted in the outfield. The grass was deep, and the ball was lost and then found, producing hilarity and cries. Inna and Sablin walked back to the cabin with their mother, who was not feeling well. She had a fever but wouldn't speak of it.

In the morning, she couldn't get up. She lay silent, breathing weakly. She remained sick all that week and missed work. Each morning, Sablin walked the path to the main house to tell the head woman that his mother couldn't work. There was no pity. Only a sigh and the threat of losing her job.

"My sister could fill in for her," Sablin said.

The head woman waved him away. "Go take care of your mother," she said.

And so Sablin cared for her, in the morning feeding her a warm porridge that dribbled down her chin. He wiped it away with a rag and offered her more. She shook her head. Told him that when she was gone, he should continue to work for Martens. He was tall now, with large hands and long arms. The lips of a girl. Soft and full. He lay beside his mother, a hand resting on her shoulder, Inna on her other side, and they were on a raft shouldered out to sea. At night there was a storm, and the thunder frightened Inna. He turned to comfort her. In the morning their mother was not moving, and he knew that she was dead. There were lice crawling out of her right ear. He shook Inna awake and they rose. He told Inna to wash up.

She turned to see the mother.

"Don't look," he said.

He walked out into the yard and dug a hole. Went back

into the hut. Inna was washing their mother. She had stripped her of her bed clothes, and she was using a cloth and a bucket of water. Her face, her neck, her chest and stomach and her legs. When she was done, she dried her gently and dressed her in her best dress, and socks and shoes. She took the only necklace their mother had and clasped it around her thin neck. She combed their mother's hair. Only then did she stand back. Sablin picked their mother up and carried her outside. Like a bird she was, nothing to her. He wrapped her in the blanket she slept with. Placed her in the hole and covered her with earth. The sun was rising red. It would be hot. The workers were running the threshers out in the field. All that day, Sablin and Inna sat beside the freshly dug earth and watched the dust rise from the machines. The sun set at seven. They remained beside their mother. At some point Sablin rose and went into the cabin and dippered water from the barrel. Drank deeply. The water was tepid. He stripped and, using the dipper, filled a pot and heated the water on the wood stove. When it was boiling, he added the tepid water until it was safe to touch. He took the dipper and washed himself. His hair, under his arms, his hands, feet, legs, crotch. He soaped himself and then rinsed. The water splashed down onto the wood floor and when he was finished, he was standing in a puddle of soap and water. He stepped outside and stood naked on the porch, allowing the warm air to dry him. Then he went back inside and put on the cleanest pair of pants he could find, and a mended shirt, and socks and shoes. He combed his hair that his mother had cut a month earlier. It was longer again, and tangled, but he worked the comb through it and when he was done, the knots and tangles were gone. He put on fresh water to heat, and went out to find Inna, who sat by the grave. He told her to go in and wash herself. He would keep watch. She went inside, and when she returned, her hair was wet and she smelled of soap. Together they went back to the cabin, and he took kindling from near the stove and some pages from a book that his father had left, and he built up a pile of wood in the centre of the cabin. Inna watched. He dropped in his mother's clothes, dirty and ragged. Took a match and lighted the edge of a grey shirt, and the flame sputtered and then caught. The kindling crackled. He found their mother's remaining clothes and fed the fire. And then the last blanket. Heaped all these things on the fire. And then a chair, and another. The weak kitchen table went in. His eyes were burning. He wanted to see the lice jump. He stepped outside, where Inna was waiting. Through the open door they watched the furnace build, and then came a soft, quick wind, and they both stepped back, and then turned and ran. When he stopped, he looked back, and the hut was consumed. The heat on his face, his eyes squinting, Inna behind him.

And this was how Martens found them when he rode his horse into the clearing.

Mrs. Martens insisted that they take Inna and Sablin in. Mr. Martens, though parsimonious, had more than a stone for a heart. Inna was given a room in the manor, Sablin a room above the stables. After all, he was unpredictable, burning down a worker's hut. Why? At night Sablin fell asleep to the sound of hooves and the shifting of the mares and the soft snorts of air. His job was to groom the horses. To prepare them for Arden and Wenig. Dandies both. They had no words for Sablin, and when they did, the words came out as orders. Once, when Wenig was displeased with the sit of the saddle, he hit Sablin about the ears. When the elder Martens caught wind of it, he beat Wenig with a riding crop. No one would hurt the boy. That was his responsibility.

Sablin ate in the kitchen with the maids. One, Elsa, took a fancy to him and gave him extra helpings of potatoes, the gravy dark and rich. Corn boiled and buttered. He had eaten butter for the first time at the pig roast, blocks of white paste into which he dug a forefinger, lifting it to his mouth, put off by the viscosity, in love with the salty aftertaste. Now here he was, eating butter and cobbed corn, his lips stung from salt. He was aware of Elsa's bare arms and the sweat on her upper lip. When she breathed, her chest rose and fell and he could smell her, much like the clean scent of the horses he curried in the evening, late, when the house and the buildings were quiet. She was eighteen at that time, a year older than him, and she touched his head as she passed him by, and she called him Little Master. He didn't call her anything, for he didn't speak, neither to the maids nor to the patriarch of the house, nor to the sons. To speak was to rise above one's place in the world. He spoke to the horses.

◧

His duties included exercising Mrs. Martens's horse, a grey mare that stood sixteen hands and was skittish because she was rarely ridden. Sablin loved this horse. Her name was Olga. When he saddled Olga, she liked to hold the air in her lungs, wait until the cinch was tight, and then release her air. "You sweet thing," Sablin said into her withers, and he kneed her. Not too hard, but hard enough. It was a game they played. Olga knew what to do, and Sablin went along with it. Olga's eyes rolled. She snorted.

"Laugh all you like," Sablin whispered. He cinched her and lifted himself up. Olga shimmied and danced.

"Beautiful girl," he said.

He followed the country roads, and on the occasions when a wagon passed, Olga rolled her eyes wildly and he had to rein her in and talk to her. But the roads were mostly quiet, eerily so, as if everyone had died and gone to heaven. Eventually he exited the road, through the ditch, and he led Olga down to the river, where they followed the stands of maples and oak. It was fall, the river was low, the bees were busy, and the leaves were turning colour. He dismounted and sat in the grass by the bank of the river. Olga grazed nearby. He was overwhelmed, full of desire, for himself, for another, for contact. He closed his eyes and found Elsa, the one with the sweat on her upper lip. Her fingernails were short from biting them, and she had down on her forearms. She was kneading bread. She touched his head, and the back of his neck. He dreamed of a bed like the one Martens owned, with wooden posts and a gossamer quilt, in a house that was large with many rooms. He owned the house. He owned the bed. He had horses. A stable. And Elsa was nearby. He opened his eyes and there was the horse cropping the grass, and the bees above, and his own hands, and his knees and his boots. He rose and mounted Olga and rode with great speed back to the stable, across the fields, and through the ditches, pushing poor Olga to the extreme, so that when they arrived at the stable, the horse was frothing and wet and he had to wash her and brush her as she trembled. He was trembling.

The following week he was called by Martens, asked to come up to the house, and he did so and found Martens in his study, sitting in his wooden chair with the leather seat and the worn arms. Behind his grand desk. Martens motioned for Sablin to sit.

Martens was wearing a white shirt and a black jacket. Black pants. Black boots. His hair had been cut recently, and there was not a strand out of place. Rumour had it that Martens loved clothes, and he loved the presentation of fine things. These were not Sablin's words, but the words of the foreman, Tolya, who spoke of Martens's taste in clothes. Of the fine things in life.

Martens asked how he was faring. "Are you treated well?"

Sablin nodded and said that he was treated very well.

"No more trouble with Wenig?"

"None."

Martens had a thin mouth, the top lip barely visible. He said that Wenig was impetuous, full of mischief, and in need of a strong rein. He said, "It is my job to provide that rein."

Sablin did not know if he should agree or speak or nod, and so he did and said nothing.

"Mother and I were talking," Martens said.

At first Sablin did not understand, for his mother was dead, and then he knew that Mother was Mrs. Martens. Annalee. He waited.

"She has become very fond of your sister. As you know, we do not have any daughters. Of course, we had Katka, and miss her dearly, especially Mother, and this is one reason we want to make Inna a part of the family. Your sister. She will take our name. She will be baptized. Your sister will be our daughter."

The boy could not breathe. Nor could he think. He only felt. Dread, sadness, perhaps happiness, and finally confusion.

"Does my sister know?" he asked.

"Mother will talk to her."

"What will happen to me?" the boy asked.

"You will take the Martens name as well. I have arranged for the papers to be legalized. All is set. Let's be clear right now, so that you don't have rubles dancing in your head. Arden is the youngest. He will gain the inheritance. Even so, you will have every advantage. I will treat you well. You will attend school. You will come to church. You will learn to read the Bible. You will be like an equal to Arden and Wenig."

"Do they agree?" the boy asked.

"It is not for them to agree or disagree. It is decided."

The boy said that he would miss the sound of the horses at night.

Martens said that the horses would still be there in the morning. "You are no longer a peasant."

He said that with great privilege came great responsibility. "You must be a good man. Fair to others. Generous, but strict. Mother wants you to change your first name. I convinced her to let you stay as Sablin."

He said that a Martens was never lazy. He did not mention his eldest son, who was extremely lazy. He said that work was all. At school, at home, in the stable, out in the fields. He said that the boy would go to school, to learn to read and write and to learn maths. He would keep his head down, he would speak when spoken to, he would eventually come to believe and be baptized, he would learn to sing, he would accept his place in the family. Did he understand?

Sablin nodded. He was still thinking of his name. He did not want to lose it. He was grateful to the patriarch for allowing this.

"Good," Martens said. "Tolya will show you your new room."

And he was dismissed.

The school he and Inna attended had been established by Martens, and it served the various Mennonite children in the area, some of them from other estates, and others the children of the landless Mennonites or the children of the workers on the estate. Martens believed education was essential, and he hired a young woman of twenty who had recently graduated from teachers' college, someone who could teach in both Russian and German.

Sablin hated school. He was seated with a younger grade, above whom he towered physically. He did not know how to read. The alphabet confused him, as did mathematics, where a multiplication sign looked like a plus sign and subtraction looked like division. He was laughed at and mocked. It was only on the playground, at lunch and during breaks, playing sports, that he excelled. He was quick and strong, and cheered for his excellence. But back in the classroom, he was ashamed. If he knew what was expected of him, he learned to prepare. For instance, if he was expected to read a passage from the Bible, he asked one of the younger children to read it to him, and he committed it to memory. When the teacher asked him to read the passage, he stood before the class and recited what he had memorized. And so, he escaped ridicule.

Inna, who had all the previous years of schooling, taught him in the evening, in her room.

He was slow. Called himself dumb.

"You are not," Inna said. "Here, look."

She began with small words, and connecting words, and she showed him nouns and verbs. She made him hold his hand in front of his mouth to feel his own breath as he pronounced words.

"Do you see the difference?" she asked.

He didn't. And then he did.

They sang the alphabet together.

He memorized everything. He began to spell in both languages, preferring German because this was the language of the estate. He began to write, and because he had memorized so many words, and written them out repeatedly, his orthography was flawless. He found that if he stroked his left cheek as he read, his comprehension was better. Inna noticed. She told him that others would laugh at him for this. "Be careful," she said.

Eventually, he was moved up to his age group, where there were all girls except for Sablin and one other boy.

He was required to attend church. This was something he and his sister had not done when their mother was alive. But now it was expected. He was given new clothes. New boots, though they were not truly new, simply handed down from H.H. But they felt new, and he was proud and pleased. The leather was deep brown, and well-worn, and soft. His boots slipped on easily, and then off again more easily. He wrapped them in a cloth at night, so they did not get dusty.

Inna wore new dresses, for there were no older girls to pass down what had been outgrown. The mother, Annalee, taught Inna how to braid her hair properly. Talked to her about her duties. Which were to God and family. Annalee wanted to be called Mother. She told Inna that she was part of the family now, and it was important to recognize the father and the mother. Inna obeyed. She was agreeable. She had become fond of the house, which had forty-two rooms in total — she had counted them — which included a playroom and a library and various large rooms with fireplaces for gatherings, and many bedrooms, and an indoor toilet. She began to take this life for granted, the comfort, the privacy, the servants who poured her bath, the meals prepared by others. She was quicker now with her answers, and she seemed to understand that she was important, and the sons, Arden and Wenig, liked to quip with her, especially Wenig, who was fascinated by her haughty looks. All that winter, while dining, or when sitting as a family in the large room by the fire as the father read from the Bible, Wenig watched her. And waited.

And then it was spring, and the calves were birthed, and the birds were back, and the snow melted, and cherry and pear trees bloomed in the orchard, and the winter wheat began to show. One day after school Wenig offered Inna a ride on his horse. She was with Sablin, walking back to the house, and Wenig rode up and blocked her path and he reached out a hand to her and he said, "Climb up."

And she did. Without question. She put her foot on top of his boot, and she took his hand, and he pulled her up.

He said, "Hold on."

She put her arms around his waist and leaned in. Wenig kicked the horse. Her hair bounced on her back. Her dress had slid up on her thighs. The horse was warm against her legs and the sun was warm on her head and Wenig's back was warm. He smelled of flower water, which was not especially appealing, but she accepted this.

Sablin was not surprised. He had seen this coming, and he had warned Inna, but Inna just laughed and tossed her hair. She was vain, but he knew the vanity was deserved, for she was above the others in her beauty and in her confidence. Perhaps it was school that had brought on this self-possession. Or the surplus of mirrors in the house. Or the admiration of the patriarch, Martens, and his wife. She was now their daughter.

That evening he said to Inna, when they were alone, that Wenig was her brother now. He couldn't be anything else.

She laughed. "I am too young for that," she said. "And he is too old for me."

"He doesn't see it that way," he said.

Inna slapped him across the head. Very lightly. He was aware of how her dress fit her.

He said, "You have no idea about boys."

She said, "You have no idea about girls."

And so it happened, that every day after school Wenig found her, and he hoisted her up, and they rode together. Wenig appeared to like riding fast, for it was then that Inna had to cling to him, and she did this readily, fearful that she would fall, and yet aware of her pleasure in holding him tightly. They rode the edges of the newly planted fields, down to the river, where they dismounted and sat in the grass while the horse ate, pulling up the green grass and then stepping down into the water to drink. Wenig swam. He threw off his clothes and he dived in. He called out for Inna to join him. She didn't look at him, at his bare chest, and his bare legs. She just slipped out of her shoes and short socks, and she pulled up her dress, and she stood in the shallow water and looked out over the trees.

"Are you afraid?" Wenig asked.

She shook her head. She wasn't at all afraid.

The water was very cold, and when she stepped back onto the shore, her feet and ankles were blue and numb.

The first time he kissed her, she pulled back and said that they were brother and sister.

He said that there was no blood between them, and so there was nothing to fear. He held her neck in his hands.

"Your father will be angry," she said.

"He won't know," Wenig said, and he kissed her again, and this time she let him.

She was in love. Or so she thought. She said nothing to Sablin, though she sensed that he suspected.

Wenig was full of pressure, but the pressure was within herself as well, and so much was possible, and if anything Wenig was surprised by her willingness. She was both in control, and out of control. Her dress was spread out on the grass, a blue-and-white bed, and she turned her eyes away from her knees, which were bare.

Come late August, during the afternoons, she began to suffer tremendous fatigue. One time she lay down on Mr. and Mrs. Martens's bed, and woke, astonished at her presumption. She never slept in the afternoon. She was not one to take naps. And then she found that she was waking at night, extremely hungry, and for two months she had not had her regular flow, which made no sense, as she was very consistent. When she realized her plight, she ran to Sablin and told him. He did not seem surprised. He said, "And you think the family will care?"

"Of course," she said. "It is their grandchild."

Sablin laughed. "You are nothing," he said. "Just watch."

Inna made plans to declare her love for Wenig, and to tell him the news. But before she could do so, banns were announced in church, declaring that Wenig Martens and Irmgard Koop from Village #3 were to be married. When Inna heard these words, she was certain that there was some mistake.

The names were wrong. The minister must have been confused. But it was true. She felt faint and wanted to run and hide. But she only stared straight ahead, at the fine and long neck of a certain Mrs. Rempel, who was sitting directly in front of her. Mrs. Rempel's husband was wealthy, he owned a window factory, and it was clear to Inna that she would never wear dresses like Mrs. Rempel, who today wore a pastel-yellow dress with a white belt that tied in the back. The beauty of the cloth made Inna incredibly sad. Irmgard and her family were invited for lunch. Irmgard was flanked by Wenig and Mrs. Martens, and at one point Mrs. Martens was holding Irmgard's hand, and they were discussing the wedding. Inna did not touch her food. She excused herself and went out in the yard and walked to the stable, where she found Sablin. She sat on a small wooden stool and watched him trim Olga's rear hooves.

He looked at her.

"What should I do?" Inna asked.

"Nothing."

"Mother should know," she said.

"You won't be believed," he said.

"But it is true."

He laughed. Shook his head. "You should have heeded me."

One evening, when Inna was in her room, Mother came to her. Her dress whispered across the floor and her voice whispered as she touched Inna's head. "You are sad," she said. "I saw what Wenig was doing, and I should have talked to you, but it seemed harmless. I didn't know that you would feel so strongly." She said that Inna was like family. "You are my daughter. But you cannot have Wenig. He is spoken for. Whatever he did to steal your heart was wrong. He is impetuous. Full of fire. Irmgard will tame him. This is for the best. You come from a different place. Do you see?"

"I didn't love him," Inna said. "Until I thought I did. And then came the announcement, and I was ashamed."

"Will you behave?" Mother asked.

"Of course. Of course. Tell me how."

"You sweet thing," Mother said. And she held Inna's hand and touched the top of her head. She said, "After the wedding you will have to leave. Irmgard has asked this of me, and Wenig as well. It won't work to have you in the house."

"Where, though? Where will I go?"

"There is a certain Julius Lehn, in Rosental. He is a bookseller. He will take you on as a maid. He will attend the wedding and so you will meet him."

"You are throwing me out?"

"No. You will choose to leave."

"And Sablin?"

"He will continue here."

Inna said nothing about the baby, and because she said nothing, she thought perhaps that she wasn't pregnant, and that she had created the story of the baby to keep Wenig. The following morning she was sick, and so once again the facts did not lie.

For two days she kept to her room, weeping quietly, pacing, angry and then sad and then angry again, but this was not her true nature, she could not exist in this way, and after those two days she decided to look about for what was good and lasting, and she found this in the garden, and in the smell of the flowers, and in her own face and figure reflected in the mirror of her bedroom. If there was to be a wedding, then she would be the most beautiful one present. She sewed herself a new dress, and she prepared her shoes, and on the day of the wedding she wore her hair down, and she chose a hat with a wide brim, and she tilted the hat back slightly so that her eyes were clearly visible. She observed the frumpy Irmgard standing beside Wenig at the front of the church and she felt sorry for the poor girl, who did not know the dirty pond into which she had been dragged.

There was a cousin from Moscow, who had flown in on his own plane, had in fact landed in the south pasture with great aplomb and fanfare. This cousin, named Grigor, descended from the plane along with his wife, a tall woman with a sharp nose and a slender neck around which was wrapped a silk scarf. She wore a hip-length tunic and a black skirt that flowed around her bare ankles, and shoes with straps that resembled a horse's harness, and it seemed that she was saying, I am a peasant, though she was the most beautiful peasant Inna had ever seen. Her ankles were bare, and her forearms were bare, and her hair flowed free, which to Inna's eye was otherworldly. Her name was Tatiana, just like the Tsar's daughter. She was Russian. She was an actress.

And with her eyes, and with her body and legs, Inna followed Tatiana around. At the wedding she sat three rows behind her and observed the back of her head and her neck — she had pulled her hair up into a chignon — and her slight shoulders. When Tatiana leaned into Grigor and whispered in his ear, Inna swooned, for she had not seen lips that luscious before. And when the congregation stood to sing, Tatiana swivelled her small head about, studying the congregation, as if she were a scientist who had discovered a new species. She smiled in an ironic manner, as if bemused, and seeing this, Inna pulled herself upright and pushed out her chin and chest and imagined that she was better than the farmers and estate owners who surrounded her.

The day after the wedding, after a good argument between Martens and Grigor about the war — Martens supported the Germans, Grigor was against war in principle — Grigor suggested that his wife might do a reading from a Chekhov play, a writer that no one on the estate had ever heard of except for Julius Lehn, the bookseller from Rosental, who had been, of course, invited because this was to be Inna's future. Inna was aware of him, and immediately compared him with Grigor, who was suave and handsome and young. Lehn seemed slightly lost, though when the reading was suggested, he called out that Chekhov would be a worthy choice. Inna looked at him briefly, aware of the timbre of his voice, and turned away.

She sat on the edge of her seat as Tatiana read from the first act, her voice projecting out over the small audience that had gathered in the reading room of the estate house. Here was something different, something new, something that opened the purse of her heart and left her gasping for air. She had heard the Bible, and she had read religious stories in school, but never had she heard language such as this. Or such humour. She applauded loudly. She laughed. She heard music. And then Mr. Lehn rose and offered a few words about Chekhov. Lehn was short, and he wore gold round glasses, and he had very little hair, and at first Inna did not want to listen to him, she wanted only Tatiana, but then Lehn called for Tatiana to join him at the front, and together they read briefly from a scene, and it was at that moment that Inna saw a different Lehn. His voice was easy to listen to — in a choir he would have sung bass — and he was playful, and obviously Tatiana liked him, for they touched each other with their hands and with the words, and when the evening ended, she saw that Lehn was more than a short, balding man in a worn jacket. She was ashamed to have judged him falsely. And when he approached Inna and introduced himself, she was happy to apologize.

"I was surprised," she told him. "You surprised me."

Lehn said that he was happy to have surprised her, and he said that he had enjoyed watching her enjoying herself.

"I did enjoy myself. Sometimes nothing happens here. And then it all happens at once — an airplane lands in the pasture, a wedding, music, the food, and then the reading by Tatiana. Who is so beautiful."

Lehn nodded. He looked her up and down. She was taller than he was, and she crouched slightly, so as not to slight him. He thought that this young woman would not care in the least what Julius Lehn thought, or wanted, or that he was interested in her. If he asked her to sweep out the oven, she would laugh and say that she would not sweep out the oven of a man who could not take care of himself.

"I refuse to be unhappy," she said.

Oh, but that line alone made her very attractive.

She said that she was adopted. And so, her last name was now Martens. Her mother had died of typhus. Her brother worked in the stables. He was here, at the wedding, but now he was probably back with his horses. He was shy. She wasn't.

"I can see that," Lehn said. He said that she was very young, and that she had the enthusiasms and innocence of the young, and then he said that it was very nice to meet her.

She was left alone. She felt that Lehn had insulted her by calling her youthful and by talking about her enthusiasms. What nonsense. He was arrogant, and old, and he was losing his hair. She decided that he was not worth thinking about, even though Mrs. Martens had said that he was in her future. She could not imagine it, and so pushed the idea away.

Over the weeks that followed, Inna wandered about the house, getting in the way of the maids, sleeping in, studying herself in the mirror, thinking of Tatiana and of Moscow and of the theatre and, against her will, of Lehn as well, who had returned to his village and his books. When she saw Wenig in the yard, or at meals with Irmgard, she wondered with astonishment how she could have been so foolish. She had chosen poorly, and now she would suffer for that choice. Lehn, upon leaving the estate, had given her a collection of stories by Gogol. She read at night, by candlelight. Someone had marked it up, little scribbles in the margins, and she thought that it might have been Lehn, though it could easily have been another reader, but she chose to believe that it was Lehn, and she studied his musings carefully, as if something new might be revealed about his character. He found Gogol funny, as did she, and so he had a sense of humour. A few days earlier Mrs. Martens had stopped her in the large hall and said, with no prelude, that Lehn was not married. He had been years earlier, but his wife had died. There were no children. Mrs. Martens said that his books were his children. "He is too fond of books," Mrs. Martens said. "But he is a good man. Not rich, but kind."

Inna said that she had no interest in poverty.

But then a letter came from Lehn, and so he was now again in her mind. He said that he had other books to send her, should she want them. Or better yet, she could come to him and choose whatever books she wanted. Come be with me, he wrote.

How is this possible? you must ask. We have only
met once. I am old. And you are young. But the
world is restless, Inna. I fear for everyone. I see with
great clarity the machine of the world. The violence.
I dislike war. I dislike guns. I have my books, I love
my books. You cannot kill anyone with a book. You
cannot kill anyone with love. I yearn for your fervour.
Your laughter. I would like to read Chekhov with you.
You should know this. I respect your decision. With
affection, Julius Lehn.

She was shaking. What an odd request. She did not know
the man. What did this mean, "be with me"? How would they
live? One of his teeth was crooked. She had noticed that. His
hands were fine, though. What did he smell like?

Just a few months earlier she had imagined that her future
was spread before her like an enormous meal. There was the
war, of course, but when it was finished, she had imagined
getting back to dressing in her fine clothes and planning for
her life, perhaps going off to Moscow to study at the university,
achieving a life like Grigor's and Tatiana's. If only. And now,
quite quickly, everything had broken up into parts, and those
parts into smaller parts, and everything was coming apart.

She wrote a letter to Lehn.

Dear Mr. Lehn,
    I accept.
    Inna

4.

FAMILY HAPPINESS

Her brother Sablin delivered her, and her one wooden crate with clothes and her effects, to Lehn's house by droshky. Sablin did not speak during the ride, except to respond to Inna's questions.

"You will come see me?" she said.

"If it is allowed," he said.

"And you will stay away from Wenig?"

"I'm not afraid of him. He won't touch me."

"I worry about you."

He grinned. Said that she should start thinking about herself, going to live with an old man. What did she think would happen.

"Nothing will happen."

"Like nothing happened with Wenig?"

She turned away.

Lehn was not at the house when they arrived. A neighbour woman followed by two girls appeared and said that Mr. Lehn was at his bookshop in Ekaterinoslav. "You're to go in," she said. "That is the message."

Later that evening this same woman brought over smoked sausage and bread and butter for Inna. She was alone. The woman called herself Mrs. Goerzen. She stood in the doorway of Lehn's small house and peeked over Inna's shoulder to survey the interior. Her daughters flanked her, Leah and Rachel. Rachel announced their names, and their ages. "I'm eight, and my sister is ten." A talker, full of bright goodwill.

"He's often gone," Goerzen said. Then she said, "He's your husband."

Inna agreed, though it wasn't true. What stories had Lehn been telling? But, of course, this was the only way they could be together in the same house. Husband and wife. Inna smiled and told Goerzen that they had been married three months earlier. The wedding had been very small.

"It's about time," Goerzen said. "He has holes in his pants. We'd given up on him."

What to do about holes? What to do about a house that needed cleaning? She had no experience. Her life at the Martens estate had been one of privilege, where food was made for her, where her clothes were washed by a hired girl, where she loitered all day and did no work, save for sitting before a mirror and admiring herself. That night she slept alone, in his bed, on sheets that had not been washed in a long while. In the morning, she woke with a singular mind and did what she had observed the servants do at the estate. She stripped the bedclothes and soaked them in boiling water and scrubbed them with soap, rinsed them, and hung them out to dry. She dusted and swept the house. Organized the summer kitchen, which was in disarray. It was late September, and there were no flowers to pick, but she found sound stalks of grass and cut them for a vase, which she placed on the table. She found an old tablecloth tucked away in a drawer. Laid that out. She hung her dresses in the large armoire in the bedroom, beside a few of Lehn's jackets and pants. She took one of his jackets and held it to her nose and breathed. Found the pants with holes and borrowed a needle and thread and scissors from the neighbour Goerzen.

Goerzen lived alone with her daughters. Her husband had been conscripted and was serving as a medic. "You are fortunate to have an older husband," Goerzen said. "He won't be called."

Inna agreed, though she had not given this any thought, that to have an older husband was a good thing. She was still, in her manner, and in her privilege, naive as to the goings-on in the world.

Goerzen asked when the baby was to arrive.

Inna must have looked surprised, for Goerzen touched her arm and said, "It is obvious to me. But then women can see these things. I know that a woman is with child within the first week. It shows in the face."

Inna put a hand up to her own face. She said that she wasn't sure when the baby would come. "At the right time," she said.

Goerzen laughed. "You'll have to prepare. I will show you."

For supper she ate boiled eggs and buns. Rachel brought the food over, and then stayed some, sitting on a wooden chair at the table, talking about her schooling. She was good at languages, Leah was best with numbers. They both sang in the children's choir. "Can I sing for you?" Inna said that she'd love to hear her sing. And so she sang, a hymn that Inna had heard in church when she attended with the Martens family. Rachel's voice was clear, and the song, "He on the Cross Is My Love," seemed too serious and too ancient for such a young voice. Rachel stood as she sang, her hands folded before her, and when she finished, she bowed her head slightly and sat.

Inna said that it was beautiful.

"It's my father's favourite," Rachel said. "I sing it for him every evening before bed. Though now he is gone. But I still sing it, as if he were at home, in the room. We miss him. He wrote a letter to say that his hair is now white. It changed in a day. I worry that I won't recognize him when he returns. He is with the White Army, he works as a medic. In his letters he describes the places he sees, the cities, the food he eats, and that he misses Mother's cooking. Mother is the best baker in the village."

"She'll have to teach me," Inna said. All was strange. This young girl in her dress and braids, talking like a little adult about cooking, and singing sombre hymns. She missed the estate.

That evening she drank black tea in the dark kitchen while a lamp burned. Shadows all around her. A dog barked in the village. A rooster crowed. She thought about where food came from. Decided they should have chickens. And a pig. And one cow. She would tell him this. There was a small barn attached to the house. It was empty, but it should have life. She slept that night on clean sheets, wondering where he was. In Ekaterinoslav, of course, but he had known of her arrival, and why was he not here?

The following day a note arrived via a shopkeeper who had travelled to Ekaterinoslav and spoken with Lehn. The note was brief, with no affection. "I will arrive Friday evening. Lehn."

He had left a few kopeks on the dresser. She used it to buy a ham hock, and some dried peas. She bought flour, and eggs, and Goerzen gave her some milk. She skimmed the cream, planning to use it for garnishing the soup that she would make for Friday. She prepared the dough for buns on Friday morning, early. This she had learned from watching an older woman in the Martenses' kitchen. But watching and doing were two different things. The oven was too hot, she had not waited for the wood to burn down to embers, and so the bottoms burned. She cut the burned parts away and laid the buns in a basket and covered them with a cloth. She boiled water for a bath and scrubbed her body. Mrs. Martens had given her some fine oils and an imported bar of soap — for special occasions — and she used the soap now. In the late afternoon she set the table for two. Then she put on the dress she had worn at the wedding and found that it was tight at her waist. But not too. Not yet. She brushed out her hair and tied it back with a blue ribbon. Finally, she sprinkled some of the fine oil on her wrists and touched her wrists to her neck, and she drew a deep breath.

She sat in Lehn's wooden rocker. Studied the leather boots that Mrs. Martens had bought for her on a recent trip to Moscow — this was when she was still in favour, when Wenig had just begun to pay attention to her, before the shame had arrived. There was a spot on the right boot, a bit of dust or mud, and she got up and wiped the boots with a cloth. Sat down again. She heard a wagon approach the yard, and then ride on. A horse neighed. She thought of Sablin. Of her mother. Of her fear, felt right now, in this moment, in this strange house, the house of a stranger, an old man, her pretend husband. She cried. Stopped crying. She yawned, and then fell asleep, and woke in the darkness of the small room, shivering with cold. She heard the clatter of traces, and the snort of a horse, and the voice of a man, and then he was there. Standing in the doorway.

"It's dark as dark in here."

She struck a match and lit the lamp.

"There you are," he said. He stepped forward.

She rose and backed up.

"Are you alone?" she said.

"Of course."

She fed him the fresh buns and pea soup with a bit of cream. He ate with fervour, looking up at her and then down at his food.

"The bottoms are burned," she said.

"Never noticed," he said.

When he had finished eating, he leaned back.

"I'd forgotten how you were," he said. "You go away and make up images in your head. And then you come back, and the image has changed."

"For better or worse?"

"Much better."

"The village thinks that I am your wife," she said.

"It's easier that way. Otherwise, people remember their morals, and they point fingers."

"It's not true."

"Of course. I know that."

"Do you wish it to be true?"

"What I wish is unimportant."

She felt dizzy. Relieved.

She said, "I patched your pants. And cleaned the house. It was dirty."

"Yes. Well."

This seemed a statement of singularity, as if to say, I am alone.

She did not know anything about his life. She wanted to know, but it was not her business. She had nothing. He had everything.

"The soup was very good," he said.

"The buns were not. I must learn to use the stove," she said. She was blushing, though he could not see.

"I am not dangerous," he said. "We are married only in title. Inna and Julius Lehn. Though it does have a ring. Don't you think? You needn't worry. I am old. You are young. You have your life before you. Everything before you. I have everything behind me."

"You sound dead."

"Only to say, I want nothing from you."

"Except buns that aren't burned."

He laughed.

"The Gogol was good," she said.

"Isn't it?" His voice went up slightly, and in the months and years to follow she would come to understand that conversations that centred on words and books always made him lift his voice slightly, and he would lean forward in his chair, and his eyes would brighten, and he would appear as if in love.

Others called him Lehn. She did the same.

There was one bedroom with two small beds. That night Lehn pushed the beds to opposite ends of the room and then hung a curtain as a divider. In the dim lamplight Lehn heard Inna prepare for bed, and if he had wished, he could have observed her through the thin curtain, the shadow of her, but he turned away. When she was lying down, they talked past the curtain. He said that during the week, when he was in Ekaterinoslav, she could come and live with him. If she liked. Or she could stay here. But she might be lonely. It would be good for him if she could help him in the shop.

"Mrs. Goerzen says that you have a woman working for you."

"True. But if you come to stay with me, she will leave."

"Is she your lover?"

He chuckled. "You're very frank." Then he said, "She is a friend."

"I don't think I would be welcome, then."

"I will ask her to leave," Lehn said.

"I don't want to be responsible for your unhappiness."

Again he chuckled. "Strange," he said. Then he said, "Tell me about yourself."

It was dark, of course, and they could not see each other, only hear the other's voice. This made talking easy, for Inna. She described her life at the Martens manor. The luxury. Her schooling. How everything was provided. The love of Mrs. Martens. The haughtiness of the father.

Lehn thought of Katka, and how life was repeating itself. "You called him Father?" Lehn asked.

"Yes. And Mrs. Martens was Mother. And two brothers. Wenig and Arden."

"Rascals, those two."

"Do you think so?"

"Absolutely. Trouble."

She was quiet.

Then he said, "We'll have to make room for the baby."

She went numb, and then was breathless, and she could not speak.

"There's a man called Hoeppner who's a carpenter. He can make a crib and add onto the house. I know nothing about tools, or wood, or building. For that reason, I am laughed at here. All these Mennonites, they use their hands, and when someone like me comes along, they don't understand. But Hoeppner, you'll like him. A man with a wife and five children. We'll ask him soon. Good night."

And he was instantly asleep. And only then did she cry. Out of relief, perhaps loneliness, fear, and certainly out of gratitude. Her body sank into the bed, and she realized that she had been as tight as the strings on Mr. Martens's violin. And now she was released, all because of the simple and plain line about making room for the baby.

◄►

They were not physical. He made no attempts. He left her alone, and because he left her alone, her fear of him receded and she began to wish that he would approach her, and then she could decide for herself. She couldn't imagine lying with him, but she wanted to be the one to choose. He read to himself at night, and one evening she asked him what he was reading. *The Overcoat*. She asked him to read to her. And so he did. And every evening after that, he picked up his book and read, and one time he asked if she didn't want to read. She was shy. But tried, stumbling over certain words. Not understanding everything. The story was both simple and difficult. She said that normally people didn't talk like this. Or even think like this. Did they? He said that Gogol was having fun with characters who meant nothing, who were insignificant. She said that wasn't completely true, because now that people were reading about these "insignificant" characters, they were suddenly important. "Akakiy Akakievitch is important to me," she said. And then she came across a description of Akakiy Akakievitch. She read it to Lehn. "And so, in a certain department there worked a certain clerk, a clerk who could not be called very remarkable — shortish in stature, rather pockmarked, with rather reddish hair, even rather nearsighted, with a smallish bald patch atop his head, with wrinkles on both cheeks and the sort of complexion that is known as hemorrhoidal." She giggled and said that this reminded her of someone.

"My hair. Is it red?" Lehn said. He had placed his hand on top of his bald spot, as if by touching he might verify the colour. The flannel blanket that typically fell between their beds had been pulled back. Inna giggled again. Her nose turned up when she was happy, and the sight of her nose, even in the dark flickering of the candlelight, made Lehn wonder how one could fall in love with a nose, which was such a singular organ when considered closely. He said that her nose was quite fine. She smiled. Did not answer and kept reading.

For two weeks he stayed with her. And then one Monday morning he said that he was going back to Ekaterinoslav. He had work to do. He did not ask her to come with him, as he had suggested. He did not say when he would return, and she did not ask. She wondered about the woman, what Lehn would do with her. She knew her name now because she had asked. Karine. When he returned, on a Friday, she had an instinct for things, and knew that the woman was still there in Ekaterinoslav, working and living with Lehn. But why shouldn't it be that way? Who would want a pregnant waif? But she felt jealousy. And anger. On Saturday evening she refused to cook. "Do it yourself," she said. And so he boiled a few eggs and ate them with salt.

"You are angry," he said.

"Not at all."

He laughed, and this made her angrier. That night he asked

if she wanted to read, and she said no. She was happy lying on her back, holding her stomach.

"When is the baby due?" he asked.

"I don't know."

"There is a midwife named Sara Kliewer. We will ask for her. She will know."

She is dipping her foot into the water of a river and Wenig is grinning up at her, lying on his back naked in the water. She is drowning in that same river, and cannot reach the banks, which are far away. She is in her grand bed back at the estate, coddled in thick blankets. Not the thin sheets she covered herself with here. She related none of this daydreaming, these flitting images, to Lehn. Rather, she talked about chickens, and within a few days he came back with four hens, which they housed in the small shed out back. She discovered that each time a hen laid an egg, there was a loud proclamation of pleasure and pride, which amused her. But why not be proud of a job well done? And then two sheep arrived, and a hog, and a cow, which she milked morning and evening, and so she now had milk and cream. She made butter.

The baby began to move, little flutters at first, and then more deliberately, with strong kicks, often at night, when she was lying on her back. One time, when the baby was very active, she heard Lehn turn in his bed, and she whispered, "Are you sleeping?"

"Not anymore," he said.

"The baby is moving," she said. "Do you want to feel?"

He came and sat at the edge of her bed. She took his hand and placed it on her belly, over the cloth of her nightshirt. Waited. There was nothing. She was very aware of his touch, and of him breathing.

"He stopped," she said.

He removed his hand. She retrieved it and held it back against her stomach.

"Be patient," she said.

And then it moved, very slightly, and she said, "Did you feel that?"

"I think so."

Bigger now. A good kick.

"There," she said.

He nodded. He kept his hand there, and in the darkness, though she could not see his face, she knew he was looking down at her.

"You're a very good man, Julius Lehn," she said.

"I don't think so. You don't know what's in my head."

"Tell me, then, what is in your head."

"To speak of what is in my head is to condemn myself. So be it. I can be cruel. I told Karine, the woman who works in my bookshop, the woman who believed that she was singularly mine, that I was now married, and I was to be a father. Why did I tell her that? Out of pity? So, you see, I can be cold and rational. And harsh. I am drawn to darkness, and this humiliates me, and when I am humiliated, I become unpleasant. I am attracted to flaws, especially physical flaws, and at some point that physical flaw becomes repulsive to me. Like a pendulum that swings, I shift between desire and abhorrence. The abhorrence is certainly towards myself, and there are only a few who are wise enough to see that. And when they see it, they laugh at me, and then I am even more attracted to them. You should know that."

She smiled. Though he could not see her smile. She said, "You have a big head."

"I don't frighten you?"

"Why? You are tortured. It has nothing to do with me."

"This is what I mean. And now the attraction begins." He said, "How do you know it is a boy?"

"I don't. I just imagine. Because it is easier. A girl's life is too hard."

"Does Wenig know? About the baby?"

She shrugged, and then thought that he couldn't see her shrug, and she said, "I don't think so. Mrs. Martens might. Though she didn't say anything. They just wanted me to go away."

He said, "Is Wenig dangerous? Spiteful?"

"He isn't smart enough to be spiteful. He is all instinct. Greedy. Ruled by the women in his life. First his mother, now his wife."

"It's best they don't know," Lehn said.

"How did you know?" she asked.

"Goerzen talked about it. Congratulated me. And I went along with it."

"So now you are married, and you have a child on the way."

"It seems so."

"People can add. I will only have been here seven months when he is born."

"Let them add. And then say something. No one will speak of it. I know these people. They have their guidelines, their suspicions, their gossip, but in the end they will leave us alone. For all their moral judgments, they are surprisingly forgiving and accepting. You watch."

She became softer towards him. Aware of him when she passed him by in the house, as if suddenly suffering from a great hunger. It wasn't sexual, she thought, because she did not feel the same languorous stupor that she had experienced with Wenig, the heavy-throated abandonment. With Lehn it was about safety and comfort and her gratitude, which was a form of affection, in the manner that a child will love and feel safe with a parent. He never touched her, only when she took his hand, or exclaimed about the baby, and called him over to come feel. And then he did so because she had asked. He was perhaps slightly afraid of her, or maybe he was afraid of himself, and his feelings, which were strong, but then redirected. What right did he have?

As for Lehn, his thoughts became dark, and he recognized the darkness as jealousy. But for what reason? She had no other, not anymore. Sometimes, at lunch, or in the morning when she turned towards him from where she stood at the stove, he saw himself through her eyes: he looked ridiculous. He had always had a terror of being devalued, and look at him now.

But she didn't find any lack of value. Quite the opposite. He was kind, considerate, sweet. He listened to her. Let her finish her sentences. He talked to her. She did not know that men could talk like this, revealing themselves. Wenig had never talked to her. He had only grunted and commanded. She preferred talk.

And then some news that came through Lehn, who spoke with Mr. Martens. Wenig had been conscripted, but he had claimed a heart problem, and so was exempted. Arden joined the army. He wanted to kill. And then was killed by a German bullet. Lehn said that Mrs. Martens was wild with grief. Inna wondered how it was that one foolish boy died and the other foolish boy lived. And how was it that fields were ploughed while men shot each other, and grain was harvested, and the neighbours' chickens were slaughtered, and babies were born, and people still went to church. Mrs. Goerzen asked Inna why she did not go to church. People were wondering. She had no proper answer. And then said that she might go sometime, but right now she was unsure.

"You should join us," Mrs. Goerzen said. "The love of Jesus will make you better."

But did she need to be better? Was she not good enough? And what did "better" mean?

◧

The baby was born when Lehn was in Ekaterinoslav. In the middle of the night her water broke and between contractions Inna managed to walk over to the Goerzens', and Mrs. Goerzen dressed and ran over to the midwife's house, and the midwife, Sara, arrived just in time.

It was a girl.

Someone alerted Lehn, who arrived early in the morning and ran into the house, leaving his horse and wagon, and he kneeled at the bed and stroked Inna's face. He did not pay attention to the baby, just to her. She said, "Look at her," and when he did finally look, he did so briefly and then turned back to Inna. The baby did not interest him, whereas Inna had eyes only for the baby. For a month there was no name for the baby, until one night, on a Saturday, when he had returned from Ekaterinoslav, she said that the girl would be Katka.

He was quiet. And then he said that he agreed.

"You have to love her," she said. "She senses your indifference, and if it continues, she will know that you don't like her, and she will not love you back."

"I love her. She is your child, and so I love her."

"Show it, then. Sing to her. Make noises. Hold her. Let her smell you. Your smell is wonderful."

She kept the baby with her in bed, and breastfed at all hours, and sometimes, when Lehn was there, and the baby would not stop crying, he came and took her and walked her around the house, singing and talking. It was winter, and he kept a fire going, and when Katka had quieted, he sat in a chair and read out loud from what he had been reading the night before, and Katka remained quiet, and Inna heard the slipping up and down of Lehn's voice, and the timbre calmed her, and she slept.

The baby had Wenig's eyes. And Wenig's nose. Everything else came from Inna. The length of the limbs, the mouth, the hair, fine and wispy, and the long head. She loved the baby because she was hers. And Lehn loved the baby as well because it led him to Inna.

If Katka was the doorway to Inna, Lehn was like a window that opened onto the world. He went away and came back with news of the war, and news of the Tsar, and news of the apathy of the Russian people towards the war, and the number of dead, and the price of grain now that the Tsar was demanding that all grain grown in Little Russia be shipped to the large cities. And people still bought books. This amazed him. One time, he said that Karine's brother had been killed. His body had come home in pieces. Karine hated the Tsar, who was foolishly sacrificing his people. And for what? Lehn said that he had warned her to be careful of what she said. The Tsar was paranoid. He had beagles everywhere.

"What does she look like?" Inna asked.

"Who look like?"

"Karine. This woman who works for you."

"No need to worry. You are more beautiful."

"How old is she?"

"Much older. She means nothing to me. She does her job and does it well."

"I think she is beautiful."

"You haven't met her."

"I would like to. But you hide her from me."

"This is what I do, Inna. I hide. I warned you about this. Do you want me? If you want me, you just have to say, and I will throw Karine out."

"I don't want you to throw her out. This is horrible. Why would you do that?"

"I am not married to her," Lehn said.

"Neither to me," Inna said.

He sat across from her and put his face in his hands. Then he looked up and said he didn't know what he wanted. She should choose. Could she please choose?

"Don't throw her out," Inna said.

◄►

In the end, Lehn did not have to choose whether to keep Karine or not, for he was conscripted into the army. He was thirty-eight. He had no idea about war or guns or the army. But he was a warm body, and so he was ordered to appear, and he obeyed the order. Inna said that he should go as a medic, like the other men in the colony who claimed their religious status as Mennonites in order to not fight.

"But I am not religious," Lehn said.

"Pretend. Convert. Get baptized. Tiessen will gladly do that."

He shook his head. Smiled. "I can't use a god who doesn't exist to save my soul. That would make me a hypocrite."

"Better a live hypocrite than a dead atheist," Inna said.

"You amuse me," Lehn said. He said that he planned to buy a new pair of boots. There was a shoemaker in the village, a certain man named Block, who was known for using the best leather, and he was an artist at what he did, and because Lehn had a bunion on the left foot, the boots would have to be made in a particular manner, considering the shape of his left foot.

He sat at the table as he spoke. Inna came to him and held his head. Pressed him against her chest. "Do you believe that boots will save you?"

"If I am to die, I want to die well-dressed. I will have my initials stitched on the top edge of each boot. *JL*."

She said, "Oh no, you won't die." But she allowed that boots were important. She liked fine leather. The smell. The look. The creak. And initials were important, for they would identify the boots.

"Exactly," he said.

"What about your shop?"

"Karine will look after it. I will go, and then I will come back."

Her affection surprised him. When she was seated across from him once again, he looked at her and thought that she might be fearful of him dying, not because she loved him, but because he was her benefactor. But that was enough. "Don't worry," he said, "you will be taken care of. Mr. Martens is aware. He will make sure you have everything."

"Arden was killed."

"Arden was foolish. I'll hide, I'll do everything to avoid dying." He paused. "It makes no sense. I will be useless."

And then he was gone, and she missed him. She couldn't have known until he left how much she waited for him. And enjoyed the times when he was in Rosental, playing with Katka, eating across from her. She wrote him. Said that she had slaughtered one of the two hogs. And together with Goerzen had made sausages. Smoked the meat. There was bacon and ham hock. Plenty left for him. Rachel came by and sang for her. Inna said that she was trying to teach Rachel a few secular songs, to get her away from the heavy and serious hymns. Katka was crawling. Still suckling. She looks for you, Lehn. I do believe so. Inna.

The letters may have never reached him. The world was unpredictable. No letters arrived from him, but she didn't blame him. She knew that they were lost out there somewhere, swirling through the air, landing in the wrong place, read by the wrong person. Perhaps someone else was right now sitting by a fire and reading a letter written to her and feeding on the words of a stranger. Well, at least his words were being read. Nothing worse than someone speaking and no one listening. And then a letter arrived, one that had been written three months previous.

Dear Inna,

My boots were stolen. And so now I wander around in a dead man's boots, looking at the feet of my comrades, seeking my own original boots, built for my bunion. I have developed an infection on my right toe. The nail has fallen off, a scablike carapace has developed, and so now I have a slight limp. If I find him, I will kill the man who took my boots. This is true. My nature has changed. All is delusion. Men

fight over carrots, and bread, and footwear. Some of
us have guns, some ammunition, rarely does one have
both. I have neither. I saw a man swinging from a tree
yesterday. He was a deserter and had been hanged.
Any notions of leaving were rubbed from my skull.
Speaking of which, I have lice, and so my hair has
been shorn and now I have only my skull, which was
quite bald before but is even more so now. I have been
reading to some of the men. They seem to appreciate
it, but I think they don't truly understand. They call
me the teacher because I have a book and I can read.
I do not tell them that Tolstoy was a count. For a time,
I was with a group that fixed the tires of the trucks
that run back and forth to the front. Now, I have been
placed with a Ukrainian corps who are headed to the
front. When men talk of the front, I picture a head,
forward-facing, on the body of a fool who is rushing
towards his death. The men around me believe in the
commune, though they have no idea what that means.
They cheered when the Tsar was overthrown, they
believe that they will go home and have their own land
and their own cow and butter to churn. Perhaps. If
they live. There is nothing here that resembles civility.
We arrived at a village yesterday and the men of the
village were killed first — for what reason I do not
know — and the women, well, after, they were shot as
well. During all of this, I found a truck tire to repair.
Amazing how the simplest act can focus the mind and
appease the moral chaos. These are not good men.
Which means I am not good either. I am changing,
by the day, and you would not like what you see. I do

not like it. It is as if I am walking down the street and
the folks above are pouring garbage down onto my
head, and orange peels land on my shorn head, and
other detritus, animal lard for instance. Have you ever
tried to wipe away animal lard from your eyebrows
and mouth? It requires effort. And much scrubbing.
I try to scrub, but I fear I am failing. Sometimes I go
into a reverie and recall my hand on your belly, or
your nose turning up, and this aids me. I have yet to
be killed. I have not killed anyone. I hope to find my
boots, though, and then I might kill. It is sad to speak
of this. I am sorry. In fact, contrary to the above, I am
quite happy. I watch the sunrise, the rooster crows out
there somewhere, my hands smell of rubber and oil,
and I try to bathe once a week. In a river, last week,
marching towards the front, I went down naked and
came up fresh. Though that was when my boots were
taken. From the riverbank. If I should retrieve them,
I will no longer take them off. I will sleep in them,
bathe in them, die in them. And then someone can
take them from me, for there is no use for boots on a
dead man. I confess, the boots I now wear were taken
from a soldier who was killed. A very brave man. He
died bravely. And I imagine that they make me braver.
I smile as I write this.

In general, my German has been very beneficial.
I do believe we are trying to kill the Germans, though
sometimes it is other Russians, or perhaps Turks, and
once I heard there were Romanians about, though I
believe we are with the Romanians. In any case, I did
speak with a German soldier. This was during a break

in the fighting. He gave me a gift of toffee, and we
had a drink, and talked about our homes, and then
we said Auf Wiedersehen and went back to our places
and resumed shooting. Though I scurried away, for as
I said, I do not have a gun. A good thing, as it can only
get you in trouble.

I think of you. I think I like you very much. I think
that I misrepresented myself. I was too cold. I did not
speak of my affection. I was afraid to be dismissed.
I must stop being fearful. Did I tell you that we
are required to march in unison? This only when a
commander appears, and we must display our prowess
for him. It is all a sham. The lines are crooked. The
men are hungry. One fainted during the march the
other day. He was beaten. Taken away. It is important
to remain anonymous. I do so by repairing tires. I am
repeating myself.

I kiss your little hand.
Lehn.

PS. I hope this gets past the censor's pencil. If you are
reading this, it did. Thank you, dear censor.

She read the letter many times, paying special attention to
the last paragraph — *I think of you. I think I like you very much.*
How was it that distance created such a tenderness? She wrote
him back immediately, addressing him by his first name.

Julius,
No, no, I don't think you are cold. I think it is fear.
We are afraid that we will be pushed away, and so we

push the other away first, to avoid pain. But the pain
comes in any case. Your letter arrived three months
late, and so much has happened, or perhaps nothing
has happened, though your life as you describe it is
certainly more significant than mine. I wake from
dreams in which I see you dead or dying, and then
I calm myself, and say that it isn't so. It can't be so.
Katka is a distraction. She is walking, so now I am
constantly stooped, chasing after her. My legs are
youthful, though. I will show them to you when you
return.

Every month I go to the district office to collect
your army payment of eleven rubles, sometimes a bit
more sometimes less. So, even when you are away, you
provide for me. I do not know about your bookstore, if
it is still open, if the woman is keeping the money from
the sales. Goerzen whispered to me the other day that
the Tsar was dead. As you say, killed. Though perhaps
not. And the family as well, down to the youngest. Yet,
that couldn't be proved. Some said they had escaped.
When Goerzen told me this, I was baking buns, and
the world took on a different shape with the news,
and the buns were like many large white mushrooms
lying on the pans. I admit it, I was stunned by the
news. Maybe sad? I don't know. All I could think of
was the cousin's wife, Tatiana, at the wedding, flying
in and stepping out of the plane with her heeled boots
and her short dress, and the scarf she wore, and for
some reason I imagined that it was the cousin's wife
who had been shot. She and the Tsar's daughter share
the same name. And so I had equated them, thought

them equal, and if they were equal, then certainly they might both be dead. I don't care about the Tsar. I care about the children, who aren't truly children anymore. They are older than me. But still. The surprise on their faces. The indignation. How could this be? I hope they are still living, as Goerzen said they might be. Hiding perhaps. The world is upside down now. And you will think it strange of me that I still ache for gold-plated cutlery and oysters on a bed of ice. All impossible to have, ever again. Some people are created to be special. Not everyone should have a dirt floor. The poor are happy that the Tsar is dead. Mr. Hildebrandt, the miller, was shot yesterday. They say that permission has been given to demolish the estates. This is all I have heard.

Do come back. Run from danger. Don't let the evil of others crawl into you. You are too good. I am going to church. I like the singing. I don't like the preaching, which sometimes goes on for two hours. Mr. Martens came to visit. Of that I have nothing to say. It was not a good visit. Why is it, Lehn, that those who have everything want more and more? My heart is afraid.

Enough. It is early in the morning. I will go milk the cow and feed the sow. I have named her Salo. And then I will make bread. Flour is hard to come by, but Goerzen has enough for both of us. She is such a help. And her daughters take care of Katka when I am busy. Katka loves them. She loves you.

You can kiss my hand any time.

Inna.

◄►

Mr. Martens had paid her a surprise visit on a Sunday in spring. He came alone, carrying food that Mrs. Martens had sent. Soup, buns, cold ham. Inna was sitting outside, Katka playing at her feet. It was warm, and the sun was falling on her bare arms, and she heard the neighbour children at play, and occasionally a wagon passed by, but for the most part it was quiet, for it was Sunday, and families were at home, napping, or preparing *faspa*. When she saw him approach in his wagon pulled by two magnificent black horses, she was startled, and then she realized that he might have news of Lehn, dire news, and she looked at his face and his eyes were smiling, so the news was not bad, or perhaps there was no news, but then why had he come? He climbed from the wagon. She had not seen him since she left the estate. Since she had been asked to leave. He stopped before her and said her name. Inna. And she said, Father. She stood. He was still imposing. Severe. She realized that she was afraid of him. Had always been afraid of him. It was Mrs. Martens who had been tender towards her. Until she wasn't.

"Is it Lehn?" she asked. "Is he dead?"

"Oh, no. Nothing like that. Have you not heard from him?"

She said that she had heard from him once. One letter.

She picked up Katka and they went inside and sat at the small table, Katka on her lap. He looked around. "You have a home," he said.

"Yes."

"And this is the little one." He leaned forward to touch Katka's head. He said, "Good day, Katka. I am Opa Martens."

Inna could not breathe. What did he mean? Opa.

"You know her name," Inna said.

"Of course. Lehn told us."

She was quiet. Her thoughts were everywhere. She said, "He didn't tell me that he told you."

"He did. That you had a girl called Katka."

"He's a good father," Inna said. "He loves her."

"You are married, then."

"Not yet. But soon. When he returns."

Martens nodded slowly. The skin around his eyes was wrinkled, and so there was always the impression that he was smiling, and that the smile was a gentle one, which is what she had noticed when he climbed from the wagon. But Inna had forgotten that his eyes were not true. It was the mouth, which was stingy. Pulled tight, as if by a string. He talked about Mrs. Martens, and her deep sadness when Arden was killed. He mentioned Sablin, who was a hard worker still, and who was engaged to a young Mennonite girl from a nearby village. He said her name, Elsa.

"I did not know," Inna said. "I am happy for him."

"Yes," Martens said. "When they marry, you will come to the wedding. With Lehn."

He was telling her what would happen. Her hands began to shake. She did not know why. And then, as he began to speak, she understood why she was afraid, and his words floated through the air, and she heard some of them, and others slipped away, but all the words he spoke were said with utter confidence, and with such sway and force that she had no response.

What she heard was that he was like a father to Inna. And Mrs. Martens had been like a mother. They had given her everything that a daughter might have received if they had had a daughter. They loved her without penalty. With all their hearts.

She had been sent to school, she had learned to be graceful, and she had been given fine clothes and every good thing. "You did not lack for comfort and luxury and schooling," he said. And then he talked about Wenig, and he said that what Wenig had done was wrong. But also, that Inna bore equal responsibility in that sin. They were two young people, and youth was full of ardency and passion and sometimes the passion flew away. As he said this, his hands slipped upwards and then landed again in his lap. He said that Katka here should have every possible advantage, as Inna had had as a young girl. The future of higher education, warmth, the comfort of family, financial support, a religious upbringing.

"She has warmth," Inna whispered. "She will have schooling."

"Oh, Inna. Think of what we can offer your daughter. Wenig and his wife cannot have children. Well, not entirely true. Wenig can." He paused. "You see?"

Inna began to cry. Katka came to her and held her hand and touched her cheek. Said, "Mama."

She wiped at her face and said to Martens, "You won't have her."

"But she is Wenig's as much as she is yours. Even more so."

"Does Lehn know of this?" Inna asked.

"He knows nothing."

"He wouldn't allow it. If he were here, he would chase you from the house."

"He isn't here. And he has no say. He isn't the father. Listen, Inna, my love. Take some time to think. I will return in three weeks. And at that time Katka will come to live with us." He rose and placed his hand on Inna's head. She didn't push him away. "It is for Katka's sake. And Wenig. And Mother."

"Mother knew. She knew. She could have kept me there. But I wasn't good enough."

"You were. You are very good. She made a mistake. Just like you and Wenig made a mistake. And now we are correcting that mistake."

"I had no choice. With Wenig. He was very persuasive."

"You chose. We all choose. Now it is time to choose again. You will choose well."

And he left. But not before picking up Katka and jostling her slightly and offering her a comb from his pocket. Katka clutched the comb and fell asleep that night with it still in her hand.

What to do? She went to visit Pastor Tiessen. Her house was on Hoppner Strasse, at the far west end. Towards the back of her own lot she could see the two windmills, one owned by Funk, the other by dead Hildebrandt. The pastor's house was at the other end of Hoppner Strasse, and she walked there, carrying Katka. It was a Saturday afternoon, and Tiessen was in the barn with his many sons, throwing hay into the loft. He took her inside and sat her down and she told him everything, while Katka crawled around, fascinated by the flowers painted on the wooden floor.

Tiessen was quiet for a bit. He cleared his throat. Clasped his hands.

"The father is Wenig, the son of Heinrich Martens," he said.

Inna nodded.

"Not Julius Lehn."

"No, not Lehn. But Katka knows Lehn as the father. And he sees himself as the father. He loves her."

"Has Wenig met the child?"

"Never."

Tiessen made a noise in his throat. He said that the birthright was Wenig's. Clearly. But that he had forsworn that birthright. "I am not King Solomon," he said. Then he said that Martens was clearly riding in the saddle.

"Can you speak with him?" Inna asked. "He might listen to you."

Tiessen shook his head. "A man like Martens, who is used to getting his way, when he has made up his mind, there is no changing it."

"What about sin?" Inna said. "Right and wrong."

"What is the sin?"

"Stealing a child from a mother's arms."

"To put the child into the father's arms. That would be the argument. I will talk to Heinrich."

"Oh, thank you." She reached down and touched Katka's head. And then her own face. And Tiessen's hand on the table. Tiessen pulled back.

"I can promise nothing. I am sorry." He asked Inna if she prayed.

"If it would help," Inna said.

Tiessen smiled. "Prayer is not a selfish request. It is being humble. Admitting your helplessness."

"I can do that," Inna said.

She left completely humbled. And worried. She had confessed what no one had known before. That the child was not hers alone, and that Lehn was not her husband, and that she was desperately alone.

Tiessen came to her two weeks later and told her that Martens would not budge. "I cannot judge," Tiessen said, "but I will tell you that my wife was horrified to hear of your situation, and she doesn't agree. Between you and me and these walls, Martens does what he does because he can. It should not be so. But it is so." He asked if Lehn was aware. "Have there been any letters?"

"One." She said that she had not spoken of it. It would only serve to distress. "Even so, Lehn can do nothing."

"When he returns, marry him. And have children. You are young."

After he was gone, she picked up Katka and walked over to Goerzen and told her. She thought that everyone in the village would eventually know, and so she wanted to be the one to tell the true story. Goerzen was furious.

"I could give Katka to you and you could hide her," Inna said.

Goerzen said that her husband wouldn't agree. Which was true. For it came out that the opinions were clearly divided between the women and the men. The men were generally for Martens, and the women were for Inna. Of course. Though it became clear that all, women and men, believed that Inna had chosen this path, and this was the consequence of her choice. The baby would live. And live well. And Inna was young.

Inna began to go to church. Lehn would have smiled at her decision. He had no religion. He believed that the soul was found in language and novels. Not in church. Inna thought that others might think she was trying to gain favour by suddenly attending church. She was. She planned to be baptized as well. Anything to keep Katka. But before she could announce her desire to be baptized, a message came from Martens that Inna's brother Sablin would visit on a Sunday afternoon, after *faspa,* and at that point she would let Katka go along with her brother, back to the estate.

She spent that week planning her escape. She would take the train down to Kherson, where one of her mother's sisters lived. She would go to Ekaterinoslav and live with Karine, the three of them above the bookshop. She would go to the cousin's in Moscow and beg Tatiana for help. Her mind babbled. She fell into a fever. Goerzen told her to behave. For Katka's sake. So, on Sunday morning, she dressed Katka in a blue dress that had small white flowers printed on the cloth. The dress showed off her chubby legs. Leather shoes. Braided her thin hair as best she could. Pinned up the braids. Washed herself. Did her own hair. For the last two days she had talked to Katka as if she might understand everything. She said that Uncle Sablin was coming to take her for a ride. It would be fun. The horses, the wagon, crossing the river on the wooden bridge. Mama wouldn't be coming this time. But it would be fun.

When she saw Sablin climbing from the wagon, she didn't recognize him at first. He was very handsome. And taller. Sablin said her name and took her hands in his. He had such large hands. And then she saw the young woman. He said, "This is Elsa, my fiancée." He drew the young woman forward. Inna greeted her. Remembered her from the estate, working in the kitchen. She was still very young. Too young. And why was she here? Why, to help with Katka, of course. She would be the female presence.

Inna was crying. Sablin was holding her, and she was beating at his chest. His arms. Trying to strike his face. He held her. Guided her into the house. He sat her down and looked around and said that she was fortunate. Such a fine house. He was speaking too much. It was not like him.

"You're here to do his dirty work," Inna said. The fiancée was peeking around his shoulder. She looked terrified.

"He's a coward," Inna said. Then she called Katka over. Sat her on her lap. "This is Uncle Sablin and Aunt Elsa," she whispered. Kissed the girl's head. Closed her eyes. Opened them and said, "They will take you for a little ride in the wagon, okay? It will be fun. The horse's bum, and the poop?"

Inna had prepared a small wooden box of Katka's things. She told Elsa that Katka liked her blanket warmed before bedtime. She liked cream straight from the pail. She was fond of butter. She liked chickens, and to gather eggs. She bathed once a week. Water not too hot. She loved gooseberry jam. Too much. But give it to her. It will make her happy. "She sleeps with me. Tell them to let her sleep with them. Under the same blanket. I am going to the neighbour's now. Don't come for me. Just go. Okay?"

She stooped and kissed Katka's braids. Okay. Okay. I love you. Love you.

She went outside and around the corner of the house and pressed her forehead against the wall. Bit her hand. Walked over to Goerzen and went in the house and sat down. She did not look outside. She clapped her ears. After so much time, Goerzen touched her shoulder and said, "They are gone."

5.

Sentimental Journey

Lehn rode the top of a train to Kiev with other soldiers, most of them Ukrainian, not one who looked like a soldier, or who seemed capable of shooting a gun. He shared an apple with a man older than him who was wearing wooden sandals. A peasant from Gulyai-Polye who kept talking about his little girl, she was three, and was waiting for him to come home. This man was already planning to desert. Perhaps he might put a bullet in his foot. If he could find a pistol. In Kiev, Lehn was billeted with a group of forty men. They were given uniforms that didn't fit. No boots. This was the revolutionary army, made up of former Whites, new Reds, and soon-to-be deserters. The officers, though they followed a new regime, were fighting the same war. Exhaustion reigned. There was some food, which consisted of boiled potatoes and weak tea and old bread. He had heard, the night before, that drivers were wanted, and that driving lessons were available. It was very easy, very quick to learn, and it was a way to escape the trenches and certain death. He went with Anody, the apple eater, to find a driving school. Anody didn't have money and returned to the barracks.

Lehn used what he had and paid for lessons, which consisted of driving a truck through the streets of Kiev, trying to avoid the other drivers who were taking lessons. It was madness. Two hours later, he was given a driver's certificate. He had managed to reach a certain speed, to not stall the engine, and to avoid pedestrians and carriages and horses and the other trucks. He liked the feel of the motor vibrating through the stick shift into his palm. He asked after a possible placement as a driver. He was told to go away. He went back the following morning and demanded a placement as a driver. He was an excellent driver. He had travelled the Carpathians in 1914. He knew mountain roads. He knew the workings of an engine. He knew how to change tires. He was safe. None of this was true. The officer in charge said, "Go back to your men."

He was sent to the front. To Galicia.

Dear Inna. The sun is shining. I eat rice kasha. I dig holes. I try to sleep. It is cold. When I do sleep, I dream. I dreamed last night of your knees.

He was in a small company of thirty men, who were situated at the tail end of a series of trenches. Their trench was in a swamp. Bags of dirt and a bit of sod separated them from the Germans. At night he could hear the Germans speaking. To stand upright was to invite a bullet in the head. Or perhaps a conversation. For this was the situation. There were two mountains. One was called Kosmachka. The Germans occupied Kosmachka, the Russians the other mountain, which seemed to have no name. Between them lay the trenches, over which planks had been laid. Before the battle, if there was to be a battle, and no one was certain that a battle would happen, though a battle was certainly imminent, the Germans became very friendly with the Russians. They fraternized. They shook hands. Sang songs. They set up a neutral brothel in a village between the lines and they shared the local women. It was important to get along before killing the other. The Ukrainian company had heard of the brothel, but they were far down the line, and had not been invited, and so their bewilderment was heightened, and they said to each other, "What is the point of being here if we can't fuck before we die?" Lehn was quite happy to not have to choose, simply because he didn't know what his choice would be. He wanted to remain loyal to Inna, and yet there was no reason to remain loyal. She was not his wife. They were not lovers. So why such faithfulness? He had no answer. His feet were wet and cold. He was constantly hungry. He was planning his escape.

One day a commissar arrived. Seeing the unkempt group before him, and understanding that they were Ukrainians, he began to talk about Ukraine, but the men shut him down. "Don't bother us with that. We are for the commune." What that meant exactly Lehn wasn't sure. When the commissar spoke, he grinned, which gave him the attitude of not being serious. But perhaps he was serious. He seemed taken aback by the men sitting in the trenches, looking up at him. As if he couldn't make sense of who Lehn and his comrades represented, yet wanting to appeal to them in some way, as if to give them good solid and friendly words before they charged towards their death. As if to say: Let's be friendly. I pity and love you. Thank you for your sacrifice. Your bravery. Have a cigarette. And then he walked off, back to his warm hut.

Lehn ached for a hot bath, and his books. He dreamed of Inna. If he made it back, he would marry her. He wrote letters. Word had it that the offensive was to start soon. At night a man cried out, "I don't want to die." The Germans must have heard him, because now they were laughing. Lehn had heard that the Germans were very clean. Even in retreat they swept their trenches. It was like Chortitza, where the streets were impeccably clean, and the cow shit was cleaned up as soon as it landed, and the houses were freshly painted, and the barns were like kitchens. His thinking was going in circles.

They went into battle at 4 a.m. the next morning. The news was whispered from above, their officer made the announcement, and the men began to murmur. Lehn had a small knife. No gun. During the first charge, moving across the muddy plain that separated the Russians from the Germans, the soldier in front of Lehn made a sound like a laugh, and he dropped. Lehn fell beside him. Saw that the soldier had been shot through the mouth. Lehn lay there. All around were moans and cries and shouts and swearing. Someone called for his mother. Lehn lay still. He believed that if he looked dead, he might be ignored. Or he might be sabred by the Germans, who did not like to take prisoners. He crawled through the mud and dropped into a German trench. It was empty, save for a few bodies. One man was lying on top of another, and they had their arms wrapped around each other, as if hugging goodbye. One of his Ukrainian comrades was in the trench, eating something from a small pot. He would eat, and then lay the pot on the back of the dead soldier. "Are you hungry?" the comrade asked.

Lehn crawled away, following the line of the trench, which was quite clean, with smooth planks for a base, and walls made of wood. A safe and warm place. Above was the clickety clack of the battle. At the far end of the trench, Lehn curled up in a ball and began to shake. He heard a low moan that rose in intensity, like a cow about to give birth, and he realized it was his own voice. He clamped his mouth with a dirty hand. He may have slept. He may have dreamed. Daylight, a beautiful sun filtered through dirty clouds high above the edges of the trench. A wooden hammer popping against wood. Again and again. Voices. A head appeared, peering down into the trench. A German helmet, a blond moustache. A gun aimed at him. A click, and the blond German said, "Shithead." The German disappeared. Reappeared along the barrel of the gun. Lehn called out in German that he was German. He had been captured, been forced to fight for the Russians, but he was German. He hadn't killed anyone.

The soldier above him smiled. Quite a handsome man. He looked sixteen. The soldier's head disappeared once again. And then reappeared, except now he was eating, tearing bread with his teeth from a large loaf. "Tell me your story," the soldier said.

Lehn said that his home was in Baden-Baden. His father and mother owned a sanatorium there. The Villa Fredericke. His name was Lehmann. Julius. He was a volunteer.

The soldier laughed. "Your German is northern. You picked the wrong area. Have you ever visited Baden-Baden?" He continued to chew.

Lehn said that his parents were originally from Hamburg. They had never truly acquired the Swabian tongue. "You see? This is why you hear the Low German in my tones." He quoted some Schiller.

The German tilted his head. "Are you hungry?" he asked.

Lehn nodded.

The soldier made a face of agreement, though he did nothing to feed Lehn. He said that his job was to shoot the Russians in the trenches and out in the open, the wounded, the almost dead, those hiding. "You are hiding."

Lehn agreed, he was hiding.

The soldier snorted. Shook his head. "Most of your comrades are dead, or on the run. Tell me. What is true? Are you married?"

Lehn said that he was.

"Your wife's name?"

"Inna Martens."

"And you have children?"

"A girl. Katka Martens."

"And where do you live? In truth."

Lehn said that he lived on a German colony, on the Dnieper. "Chortitza," he said. "In Ukraine."

"Ukraine is beautiful," the soldier said. "The grain."

Lehn agreed.

In the distance there was a shout. The young soldier put his finger to his lips and shook his head. "Don't speak," he whispered. "Go back to your wife." And then he aimed his pistol and fired. This time the gun worked.

When Lehn opened his eyes, it was quiet. The voices were gone, the knocking of wood was gone. He heard flies. He sat up. His feet were bare. No boots. He didn't think he was dead, which was a complete surprise. Or perhaps he was, and it was in heaven that boots were not needed. He lay down again. Just in case he was alive. A plane flew overhead. The cackle of gunfire far away. The bullet had gone through his abdomen. He knew it had exited because he felt the hole with his fingers. Surprisingly little pain. Just blood. He felt dizzy. He stuffed the two holes with his shirt that he had ripped up. He lay there until night came and then crawled from the trench and worked his way past the German front. He used his German. He wore a German helmet. He took off the helmet in that place they call no man's land, the space between the Germans and Russians. Stumbled into a trench where six Russian soldiers were cooking a meal. They looked at him, saw his wound, and called for a stretcher. He thanked them.

The sky was green. Again, he believed he was dead. A woman's head appeared. It wasn't Inna. The head covering of a nurse. She washed him, talked to him, told him that he would live, and he fell in love with her. For three weeks he lived with the vision of the green ceiling of the field hospital, and the face of Olena, the nurse he loved because she washed him and talked to him. Beside him was a man who had been castrated by a bullet. The soldier knew, Lehn knew, Olena knew, but it was not generally discussed. The man without a penis would sing sometimes in the evening, songs about broiled chickens. Singing kept him from weeping.

Also, there was another soldier who had been shot in the abdomen and survived, like Lehn, and was now walking about and word had it he would be going back to the front. He was a very young man, quite happy to be alive, and apparently pleased to be going back to the war. Olena flirted with him. They had a thing. Lehn wasn't jealous. Let the boy have his last love before he dies.

After three weeks, stomach still healing, but strong enough, Lehn left the field hospital and deserted before being sent back to the front. It wasn't even a choice, and if you aren't truly choosing, if something happens spontaneously, then how can it be called desertion, which is a singular act of cowardice. He wasn't a coward. He had gone into battle and survived, and this was enough. It was simply chance. He hiked a road that curled towards Stanislau. Cars passed. Wagons with guns heading to the front. He did not look up.

In general, soldiers who have deserted all look the same. They walk in the wrong direction, with heads bowed, sometimes without shoes, no guns, ragged clothes, and there is a furtiveness to their movements. Sticks are used for canes, as many suffer from conjunctivitis. Their eyes weep. They do not see well. Deserters also find each other, though they would never admit to deserting. They claim they are sick. They have been released. They are on leave. Lehn found that he had collected a motley group of twelve or so men who were all heading away from the front. Like resolute ants, they walked single file, sometimes passing one another, rarely speaking. Perhaps they had faith in numbers. Perhaps they hoped they resembled a small company on leave. The group was halted on the road entering Stanislau. A Russian officer climbed down from a truck. Two soldiers flanked him.

The officer spoke in a voice that went up and down, and then he stood on his toes, leaning forward, and he pointed at the deserters, and he called them shit. Pure shit. One of the deserters, an older man with rags on his feet, stepped forward and put his finger against the chest of the officer and said, "Pockets for rubles from the bourgeois dogs. Beat him up." Two men leaned in, waving sticks, ready to do as bidden. The officer wasn't afraid. He raised himself up and gave a long and winding speech that was full of vitriol and insults towards the deserters, and he talked of the motherland, and he spoke of freedom, and he remonstrated against cowardice, and he said that even if they hung him up, even as the noose was around his neck, he would still call them scum. The men listened. They loved the speech. They got excited. They hoisted the officer on their shoulders and marched him around the truck. They said they would go back. For the motherland. For Lenin. For the commune. The officer climbed back into the truck. As did his two soldiers. Cheers all around. The truck departed, gears grinding. The men waved their fists at the back of the truck. "Off with you bastards," they cried. "May your feet rot as ours have." And then they carried on up the road, away from the front.

Lehn fell out with the group after this. The personality of a crowd terrified him. It was beast-like, irrational, easily swayed by passion, governed by instinct, and inclined towards death. He stayed for two weeks with an old woman in her tiny hut at the edge of Stanislau. He had entered thinking it was empty. And then she appeared out of the darkness, stooped, half-blind, and he said his name and said that he would not hurt her. Did she have food? He mimed eating. She waggled a hand and drew him in and fed him. She gave him a small cot to sleep on. He found wood for her and built her fires. He drank coffee ground from barley, tea of birch sap. At her bidding he throttled one of her old layers and plucked it and she roasted it along with some root vegetables. They ate across from each other, not speaking. He grunted in pleasure. He did not know her name. She showed no interest in him, though she seemed to appreciate the help he offered. The tending of the coals, the washing of the few dishes, repairing a window. Early on, she made poultices for his wounds, and she placed them on his front and back, shaking her head and muttering. He gave her some rubles when he left. She gave him a clean shirt and trousers, which had been her son's. The son was dead. Killed a year earlier in the war. She told him this early on, in her Galician tongue and with certain sad gestures, and though the language was foreign, he understood. When he left, she gave him some sugar wrapped in a cloth, and a piece of bread, and leather gloves, which of course had been her son's. He refused them. She forced them upon him. He took them and put them on. How light, how smooth. He smacked his hands together and at this she smiled and then turned and disappeared.

On the road he caught a ride with an ambulance truck heading for Czernowitz. He told a story of being shot and left to die and finding his way to a peasant's hut, where he miraculously recovered. He had been an ambulance driver as well. And an attendant in a field hospital. There were four soldiers on stretchers in the truck, and he set to helping with them, to prove his skills, which were few. He learned through imitation and pretending. There was a boy of seventeen whose back was broken, and he would certainly never walk again. Lehn held his hand and talked to him and told him that soon he would be galloping across the steppes on his horse. The boy said that he didn't have a horse. Didn't know how to ride. "Will I die?" the boy asked. "Will I see my mother again?" Lehn told him that his mother would be very happy to see him. Soon. The young man died just as they reached the hospital in Czernowitz. Lehn was given the uniform of an attendant, and he spent the next weeks working alongside captured Austrians, who were clean and efficient, much better than the Russian medics, and terribly happy to be away from the front, working as prisoners of war. They didn't want to return. He spoke German with the Austrians. One day a Ukrainian nurse asked him where he had learned German.

"From my wife," he said.

"She is waiting for you," the nurse said. Her name was Marta.

"She died," Lehn said. "Many years ago."

"You are still young," Marta said.

"Not so young." He took off his wool cap to display his bald head.

Marta smiled and said that she knew a young man of nineteen who had no hair.

He slept in a small room attached to the hospital, and in the evenings he walked the streets of Czernowitz. The city was crowded with soldiers in retreat, many of them drunk, a few of them violent in their gestures and language, most of them surprised to be alive. News had it that the Germans had counterattacked and were pushing the front eastward towards Czernowitz. Soon, thought Lehn, everyone will be speaking a different language here. The victor imposes his own tongue and ways on the vanquished. He saw Marta in the street walking arm in arm with a Russian soldier who had a strong chin and wide mouth. Lehn nodded and tipped his hat. Marta wore a dress that fell just below her knees, and he saw her calves, and her shoes, leather and heeled. She walked with such conviction. He admired her hips, had admired them when working beside her. That night, alone in his room, he saw Marta above him, and his hands were on her hips, holding tight. If only he had a strong chin and wide mouth.

That same night he wrote a letter to Inna. Their communication had been sparse, and her letters did not arrive in sequence. She did not speak of his news, and he wondered if she had heard from him. He imagined the censors were cutting up his letters, in which he had been far too forthright. He decided to write a different kind of letter. He told Inna that he was in the city of C., and he was an orderly. I have soft fingers, so naturally I am a medic. In general, one follows the other. He wrote that he was very proud of the Russian army, and he believed that soon the war would be over, and that soon the Germans would be defeated. Long live the government, he wrote. Long live the commune. Brusilov is the greatest general. He will prevail. Long live the Jew, in particular the intellectual Jew, who can convince the Russian peasant with his words. Long live Kerensky. Long live the Supreme Commander. Fuck the Bolshevik. Long live the Bolshevik. The Russian army is made of many small heads, the heads of soldiers, and these sad heads are crumbling beneath the weight of death.

He tore up the letter and burned the little pieces in his ashtray. He smoked. He realized that though he would say whatever was necessary to stay alive, he did not know what must be said, or proclaimed. He decided to keep his mouth shut.

In the morning, on the burn ward, Marta found him and said that there was a certain commissar, badly wounded, who required an attendant to travel with him to Petersburg.

"I like it here," Lehn said. "I don't know Petersburg."

"It is a beautiful city," she said. "You must go."

"A holiday, then," Lehn said. "Why me?"

"You are like him," Marta said.

Lehn thought, So the commissar is a Jew. He said, "I am not a specialist. I might kill him."

"To help with his bath, his ablutions, his toilet, his walking. To talk to him. To keep up his spirits. Use your humour."

He would miss Marta's hips, and her voice lilting and soft on the other side of this or that dying man's bed. Most were dying. And in the middle of all that death, her voice whispered. He didn't want to leave her.

He agreed. Because she had given him the command. Of course, Marta. Of course. May we meet in heaven. She was religious. Had told him so. And so, everything was possible.

The wounded commissar was a man called Shklovsky. Lehn got busy. Packed a bag. Arranged for transportation to a hospital train, in the car for the most seriously wounded. Shklovsky on a stretcher, Lehn sitting on a stool by his side. Call me Viktor, Shklovsky said. The first day was long. With all the stopping and starting, they travelled only seven miles. Lehn recognized the commissar as the same man who had visited the trenches on the front. The man who tried to befriend the Ukrainians. Lehn did not speak of this. He kept quiet. In a lucid moment Viktor asked him what he was. Lehn was confused for a moment and then said that he had been a bookseller. He had a shop in Ekaterinoslav. "Though perhaps it no longer stands. Who knows?"

"Ahh. Yes." Viktor was weak. He had an internal hemor-rhage. He might not make it. Lehn tried to distract him from his suffering, even though Viktor did not complain. Rumour had it that this Shklovsky had received a Cross of St. George from Kornilov. Lehn wondered if he should mention this and decided no. Viktor was too self-effacing. He carried the weight of the front. He wanted only success for the army, and the army was running. It turned out that Viktor had read many books. More than Lehn. He said that writing about war was very dif-ficult. "Of all that I've read, the only thing I can remember as a plausible description of it are Stendhal's Waterloo and Tolstoy's battle scenes. To describe the mood of a front without resorting to false and artificial passages is just as hard."

He fell asleep after this. And woke to ask for water. A bit of soup, which Lehn helped him with. Lehn spoke of the day that Gorky was supposed to visit Ekaterinoslav, of putting all of Gorky's books in the window, on display, about his assistant, Karine, dusting the books for weeks after, peering out the door to see if Gorky was arriving.

Viktor laughed. This was a fine story. He said that Alexei Maksimovich Gorky was a friend.

Lehn was astonished. "I admire him."

"Yes. A very important writer. I have been at Gorky's place many times. He laughs a lot. He has absolutely no faith in humankind, but as a man, he has the largest heart."

Perhaps because of the familiarity of the setting, the lowly circumstances, Lehn believed that he might speak freely. He said that he preferred Chekhov and Tolstoy to Gorky. Though Tolstoy liked to go on and on about the peasant. It affected reason. It evoked pity rather than compassion. Coldness was necessary. Like Chekhov. Though "Alyosha the Pot" by Tolstoy bewildered him for its emotion. Such a simple life, such a simple death. Told so clearly.

Shklovsky smiled. He said, "It takes Tolstoy three pages to reveal the life and death of a young man. A man with a small brain, mind you, and a fawning nature, but completely sympathetic. The army is full of young men like Alyosha the Pot. It is necessary. Young men are easily persuaded. They see themselves as invincible." He said that in Stanislau, in June, the Kinburg Regiment had become restless and decided to attack without waiting for the complete destruction of the enemy barbed-wire entanglements. "From the roof, I could see through binoculars small grey men running out of our trenches and crossing the field. At first our men appeared in separate sectors; then the whole winding line of our attacking troops stretched across the whole front. I wept on the roof."

Shklovsky said that if he himself were to write about the

war, it would be in the form of a journal. All would be true. The facts. But form was utmost. He would call it *A Sentimental Journey*. "Do you know it?" he asked. "Sterne?"

Lehn nodded. He had it in his bookshop, though he hadn't read it. He did not tell Viktor this, thinking that the commissar would be disappointed in him.

"Ahh. Nothing wrong with borrowing a title. Or much else for that matter. Just confess to the borrowing." And then he talked about the structure. And the absurdity. And the lack of coincidence. "Coincidence is given too much credit in novels. Though war is full of coincidence. Have you noticed? For example, you a bookseller and now an attendant for a commissar who is a writer. For that is what I am. A writer first and foremost. You don't believe me."

Lehn said that no, of course he believed him. He was certainly good with language. Though coincidence was easier to accept in real life than in books. And he told him about Badenweiler, where he and his wife Katka had stayed at the Villa Fredericke, on the second floor, in a private room. And below was Chekhov. He spoke of the death of Katka, and the death of Chekhov. He had not known. And would it have made any difference if he had known? He did not know. When he finished speaking, he saw that Viktor had fallen asleep.

When Viktor woke, the train had still not moved. Viktor said that they would find another way. "Help me." Lehn guided him off the train and Viktor flagged down a passing truck. His uniform, his insignia, gave him clout. Lehn was amazed. They rode with the troops for a time and then in hospital vans, and then with the retreating artillery, lying on shells in the back of the truck. If Viktor suffered, he did not say. They took the high road above the Dniester and arrived in Kiev via Mogilev.

In Kiev, Lehn felt the pull to go south. His head was uncertain. Shklovsky was healing, but he still required Lehn, not only for his physical needs but also as a vessel into which he might pour his passions and theories. They rode north on the floor of a train compartment to Petersburg with other soldiers, some wounded, some whole. One soldier played guitar. Shklovsky wrote in his notebook — he wrote in it often. And when he finished writing, he talked to Lehn as if they were equals sitting down to dinner and various ideas. Though they weren't equals, because Shklovsky was brave and remained in the army, while Lehn was a coward and a deserter. One night, when most of the men were sleeping, Shklovsky talked, and as he spoke, Lehn thought that someone overhearing Shklovsky's opinions might easily turn him in as a traitor. He was very clear. Very straightforward. Full of resignation. He said this: "The army is like a factory, where the worker does very little, but if he stops doing that little, the result becomes disastrous. The Russian army was ruptured even before the revolution. The Russian Revolution has freed the army from all constraints. There are no laws left in the army — not even rules. But there is a complement of trained men, capable of sacrifice, capable of holding the trenches. Even without constraints, a short war is possible — a blitzkrieg. It so happens that at the front the enemy is a reality; it's clear that if you go home, he'll come right behind you. In any army, three-fourths of the men don't fight; if there had been troops in this war that fought as well as men work for themselves, they could have not only attacked Germany but gone across Germany into France. We are losing because of the foul, ruthless policies of the Allies. I'm not a socialist. I'm a Freudian. A man is sleeping and he hears the doorbell ring. He knows that he has to get up, but he doesn't want to. And so he invents a dream and puts into it that sound, motivating it in another way — for example, he may dream of church bells. Russia invented the Bolsheviks as a motivation for desertion and plunder; the Bolsheviks are not guilty of having been dreamed. But who was ringing? Perhaps World Revolution. Why does the army take the offensive? Because it is an army. For an army, it's no harder to take the offensive, no harder psychologically than standing still. And an offensive is a less bloody business than a retreat. The army, feeling its disintegration, can't avoid using its strength in an all-out effort to end the war. The offensive won't succeed because of political circumstances. The units are already 'falling asleep'; they escape into Bolshevism the way a man hides from life in a psychosis."

Shklovsky stopped talking. He stared off into the distance. He whispered, "What about the blood of those who accepted death among the cornfields of Galicia, the blood of my poor comrades."

And then he talked about art. Or was it art? Art and the story. Something like that. Lehn was tired. But he listened because he was curious, and his scalp tingled. He would never meet another man like Shklovsky, who cared equally for both war and books. Shklovsky said that war was chaotic and incomprehensible, and then, if seen from a distance, say from above, the patterns became clearer. There was repetition, parallel movements, a lack of chronology, timelessness, more repetition, jumping around, no beginning or ending, and yet the apparent lack of structure was a structure in itself. War existed. It wrote its own plot, even though that plot was some-times nonsensical, or circular.

"You see, Lehn?"

Lehn nodded in the darkness. No answer was required.

Shklovsky fell asleep.

Lehn lay down beside him, but he could not sleep. Shklovsky had offered Lehn a copy of *Hadji Murat* to read, but he only held the book and stared into the darkness. He knew the story, had read it the year previous. Tolstoy had finished writing it in 1904 — the year Katka died, what synchronicity once again — but for censorship reasons the book had just recently been published posthumously in its complete form. The story was about power and deception and brutality. The strong conquering the weak. The cold viciousness of the Russians in the story was unforgiving. Tolstoy was very clear in his description of the Chechen Muslim repulsion, disgust and perplexity at the senseless cruelty of the Russians. And the Chechen desire to exterminate the Russians, as one would rats.

In Petersburg, Lehn delivered Shklovsky to an infirmary where Shklovsky was told by a doctor that he would live. They parted, not as friends, but as comrades on different rungs of society. Though perhaps they were equals, for Shklovsky kissed him and wished him good luck with his bookshop. Told him to read Sterne. "I hope you see your wife soon," Shklovsky said. Lehn had talked briefly about Inna, and called her his wife, for the sake of simplicity, not to complicate his story.

Lehn left Petersburg and rode the train back south towards Kiev. Shklovsky, in his kindness, had written him a note, giving him leave for one month. Well, this was not true. Lehn had observed how Shklovsky signed his papers, his "style," and he had gotten his hands on some paper with official letterhead, and had written his own letter of leave, and had signed it using the commissar's name. No one would know. Certainly not Commissar Shklovsky, who, because he was a patriot, was heading back to the front, and would likely not survive. And this saddened Lehn, to think of a man whose goal seemed to be to write his memoirs, a man who wanted to create a Society for the Study of Poetic Language, heading back towards certain death.

From the window of the train, small villages on the slopes of the mountains, some woods, spruce perhaps. Long lines of supply sleighs on the road. The train stopped and started. Young officers sang songs, and even younger women joined in. They appeared to be together. The officers got drunk and there were fist fights, some good-natured, some not. Lehn tried to blend in, to not be noticed. An officer with a large red nose approached him and asked for his papers. He said that he did not have papers, but he did have a letter from Commissar Shklovsky, a brave officer whom he had just delivered to Petersburg, and who had just received a medal of bravery from Kornilov.

The officer said he did not care about Shklovsky or his medal. Lehn reached into his pocket and produced the letter. The officer swatted it away. Lehn bent to retrieve it. The officer said that all deserters should be shot. He fumbled for his pistol. Lehn offered to buy him a drink. "Please. It would please me." The officer smacked Lehn on the shoulder and said that of course they would have a drink, and when they were finished drinking, he would shoot him. Or flog him. "How about that?" Lehn agreed. He bought a bottle of vodka from a woman at the front of the train. He had noticed her selling spirits earlier. Two glass teacups were provided. He returned to the officer and sat down and poured out the vodka. Generously for the officer. They drank. And more vodka was poured. Lehn talked and talked, about the front, and about Shklovsky, and about the Germans who shared their brothel. The officer smiled, his head nodding. Lehn told him about the duel between two men who were in love with the same woman. This was a story, amended and abbreviated, taken directly from a Russian folk tale, the kind of story that exists for its gallantry. The officer, if he knew the story, did not recall it, and in any case he was too drunk, and he eventually fell asleep with his head against Lehn's shoulder. Lehn managed to slip away from the officer and got off at the next stop. He waited for ten hours and finally found standing room on the next train, and so he continued south towards Kiev.

Lehn went from Kiev down to Ekaterinoslav, where he found his bookshop boarded up and dark. The windows of the shop had been broken, hence the boards. Some books were missing. A few lay on the wood floor. He picked these up and brushed them off and placed them in stacks on the table. The money box was gone. He surveyed his room upstairs. No bed. No dishes. Surprisingly, his axe was still leaning in the corner. He went out into the streets looking for wood. People walked furtively, heads down. Shops were shuttered. Army units passed by in trucks and wagons. He ducked into the shadows. Found no wood. He returned and chopped up one of the chairs and built a fire, for kindling using the pages ripped from a book, wooden in its writing style, that he felt he might sacrifice. He slept on the floor, long and hard, and woke cold to a dead fire. He burned the rest of the book and the remains of the chair. He found the neighbour and asked after Karine. She had disappeared just after the bookshop was broken into. The neighbour added that most of the shops had been attacked. "You were lucky to be gone. Some of the owners were hung. Or shot." The tone in which the neighbour told this story seemed slightly slanted, as if excited.

That evening Karine appeared. She found him upstairs. She called him by his name and went to him and held him. He kept his arms at his side, wary of who she was.

"Lehn. You are here."

"And you. You are back."

"I have your money," she said. "I took it and hid it when I ran. I heard you were here. It's not safe for you." She had a basket, and in it was warm bread and some jam and butter. He sat and ate. She touched the back of his head. His face. She had aged. There were lines at her forehead. Her hair was short now, tinges of grey. Her hands were raw-looking. But he saw her.

"I am with my mother now," she said. "There is little food. No one knows what is happening or who is winning."

"We are losing," Lehn said.

She did not ask him about the war, or what he had done, or how he had survived. And he had no interest in talking. They lay side by side, in their clothes, holding each other for warmth. Lehn thought of the planks across the ravine that led to the shared brothel. But this was not that. This was Karine. In the morning, returning from the market with tomatoes and bread, Karine announced that there was a dead man hanging from a lamppost in the street below. "People are anxious," she said. "It's dangerous. You shouldn't go out. Go back to your village, where it is safer. Where your wife is."

Word came that Russia was withdrawing from the war. Celebrations. Bewilderment. Mayhem in the streets. Who was now in charge? The Germans were still advancing. So be it. Perhaps they could clean up this country. Sweep the streets. Bring order.

Lehn wanted only to live quietly, with his books. He had not killed anyone. He had not cheated anyone. A book is a book.

You buy it and you read it. I will charge you what it is worth, and usually I will charge you less than it's worth. For a book can be priceless. The peasants had no idea what they were turning against. The goal was to destroy the kulak, the landowner, the bookshop owner. Heads would roll, and anything that those heads had produced, including books, would go as well. Lehn was appalled. He saw danger. He smelled fear. He had believed that selling books was an innocuous trade. The first question he should have asked himself was what class he belonged to, his origin, education, profession. Hence, his fate. He was doomed.

For the next three days he hid in the upstairs room. Karine brought him food. He burned the firewood she had found, and when they ran out, she went down into the street to seek more. She was not frightened. She opened the doors in the afternoons while Lehn stayed upstairs, where he blackened his hands with grease supplied by a mechanic friend. If questioned, he was a man who repaired truck engines. He now knew something about engines. He could drive. He started to grow a moustache, to appear as a worker. He wore a worker's cap to hide his bald head, which he believed was the sign of an intellectual. Karine laughed at this. She took his hands and held them and stroked the pads of his fingers and declared them soft. No calluses to be found. In the evening he rubbed his fingers against the bark of a log until they were raw, and then he wrapped them in cloths and suffered a little.

A week later he said that he would be going home. Karine's blue eyes turned to grey and then green. She wouldn't say if she was sad. But of course, she would take care of the shop. He hired a man to take him by wagon to Rosental. There was ice on sections of the Dnieper. The streets of Rosental were the same, clean and simple. It was like another country. He climbed from the wagon and entered his house. He listened for the sound of a child's babbling, Inna's voice. It was quiet. He found Inna in the barn, bent over, feeding Salo the sow. He watched her. And then she turned and saw him. Clasped her hands. And said his name, "Julius."

◪

Upon his return they still slept in separate beds, a curtain dividing them. The price of a pud of grain had increased four times that year. Those from the village at the edge of the colony were now more brazen, sometimes stealing eggs from the coops or walking into houses in the middle of the day and taking pillows and curtains. Not often, but it happened. Herman Wall, the miller, announced that he had acquired a seven-shot Nagant revolver. Inna wondered why seven shots when only one was essential to kill someone. Did they need a gun? Lehn said no, that meant certain death, and it was obvious that the villagers needed eggs and pillows. Inna insisted that they plant a garden. That they plant their own crops rather than let out the land. That they get Rempel's bull for the cow and give her a good load. Inna could be frank sometimes. Lehn said he didn't know how to till, or plant, or harvest, or help a bull with a cow. Inna said that she would teach him. She worked from morning till nightfall, constantly moving, rarely talking, focused on husbandry, and planting the seeds she had received from Goerzen. She was leaner, her biceps were strong. Her focus in the evenings was currying her one sow, Salo, wiping her down with a bit of heavy cream skimmed from the jug so that her hide shone. Clean the hooves, rub them with beeswax. Inna had started her own colony of honeybees, getting advice from old man Hamm, placing the hives at the edge of the apple orchard. Lehn thought that Inna was grieving, and that constant work was her way of avoiding the sadness. She worked right until the moment she climbed into her bed, and within seconds she was sleeping. He no longer read to her in the evenings.

One morning he walked through the door from the kitchen to the barn and found her milking the cow, her cheek and forehead pressed against the cow's stomach, her eyes closed. If her hands had not been moving, it would have appeared that she was sleeping.

He said that he had been thinking. He waited. She kept milking. "I've been thinking that we should get married."

She kept milking, though her eyes were open now, and this gave him courage.

He said that of course he was older and she was younger and in general she could have the pick of the various tomatoes ripening on the vine, and perhaps she already had her eye on a young tomato, and if that was the case, he would be very happy for her, though he would be sad for himself, but should that not be the case, and if he was the preferred tomato, then they should get married sooner rather than later, because it was essential that she have another child, and that that child be theirs, not someone else's. He said that she was sad, and he didn't like it when she was sad, and perhaps she didn't even know that she was sad. Did she? He knew that she missed little Katka, as did he, but of course she was the mother, and he couldn't know the emptiness, not like her, but wouldn't it be worthwhile to replace that emptiness? He said that they had confessed their love in the few letters they had received from each other while he was gone, and perhaps those words were written in a time of distance, and didn't have the same meaning now, but he thought they did mean something still, at least for him. He said that the world around them was upended, and who knew when it would right itself, but in the little circle of their home, in this garden they called home, even though he was perhaps too ripe, would she pick him?

She had finished milking. She took the pail and stood. She looked at him. She said, "There is no other tomato. I pick you." She said that she didn't want a church wedding. Maybe no wedding. They had lived together easily like this, why not continue? Everyone around them in the village thought they were already married, they had done a fine job of pretending, and she didn't care about what the Martens family thought, they had lost any right to judge.

"And about children," she said. "We will see what happens."

She reached out her hand to him. He took it and shook it as if they were settling a transaction.

She laughed. "Kiss my hand," she said.

◄►

For the wedding they would celebrate with a meal. She made fresh noodles, and she cooked sausage, a cream gravy from the drippings, and she cut fresh cucumbers. She wore the dress that she had had made for Wenig's wedding. It fit more loosely, and there were a few moth holes near the hem, but it was still fetching. She combed out her hair and let it fall over her shoulders. He wore black wool pants and black suspenders and a white shirt that she had pressed for him. Black boots on his feet. Shaved himself in the late afternoon. A small cut on his chin that he dabbed at with a cloth, until he stopped bleeding. She still had the heeled boots given to her by Mrs. Martens. Wax aglets. Lace hooks. He kept glancing at her bare calves.

He was full of joy. She perhaps not as much, though how would he know? Sitting across from her, the lamp flickering, her hair shining, he talked and talked, and they ate, and he talked some more, because he was nervous, because she was quiet, because she still had that air of sadness. He told her stories of the war. Not about death, or fighting, or killing, but about the people he had chanced upon, and the strangeness of those people, the soldier with a potato for a nose, who was very ugly, but very funny as well, as if the nose made it necessary to tell a good joke, and he told her about the commissar who was friends with Gorky and was writing a memoir called *A Sentimental Journey*, and about the young men singing on the trains, and every time he added one more story, he made it seem that war and the going to war and the coming home from war was like a holiday where every person was convivial. He wanted her to think that. What else to do? Tell the truth?

And at some point, after a long silence during which he watched her eat and imagined touching her head and her mouth and her ears — he didn't allow himself to picture her naked — in any case, at some point she spoke of the day Katka was taken. She described braiding Katka's hair for the last time, and Katka's chubby legs on the carriage bench beside Uncle Sablin, and she talked about the white dress, which Inna had sewn for the journey, and she said what Goerzen had told her, that it was necessary to keep Katka happy, for what would be the purpose of sadness, other than to destroy Katka. So she lied, and convinced Katka that this was simply a little trip, and then Katka would return. Back to her mother. Still, Wenig was the father, this was the truth, and it was good that Katka was with her father, and it was good that Katka had every privilege imaginable. "I think of her scrubbed clean from hot baths. I think of her learning to play piano. Of her warm. Of her safe. Of her surrounded by the love of family. This is how I think."

She said that she had been invited to visit. Her brother would pick her up. In fact, one Sunday, the first visit, she was all dressed and prepared and waiting for Sablin, and then he arrived in a beautiful carriage pulled by two magnificent black horses, and it was only when she saw the finery of the leather traces that held the horses that she realized she couldn't. And so, she said no. And sent Sablin back to the estate. Because what was the point? To make the Martens family feel better? To make everything seem normal and right? And what about Katka? She would suffer once again. "I'm not strong. I have never been strong. I am spoiled. I like objects. Fine things. I would ache for my old home. I would not have been able to say goodbye to Katka once again. It would have been chaos. I would have thrown a tantrum. Scratched out Mrs. Martens's eyes. There was nothing to be done."

She stopped talking. And then she laughed. She said, "Look at Mr. Lehn. Nothing to say. Have I frightened you?"

Before he could answer, she said that she would tell him what she saw when she looked at him. In this kind of light, this half darkness, he was quite handsome. His mouth was most attractive when relaxed. He had a generous mouth. And his head was a fine, smooth egg, which was a good thing because there was nothing worse than a misshapen head on a bald man. She liked his high forehead. It went on like a field stretching out for versts. She laughed. She said his voice was what seduced her at first. Way back at the wedding. And the Chekhov play. She had been surprised at how clean his voice was. "Perhaps I fell in love with you then. With the words coming out of your mouth. That you are indifferent to God and religion, that interests me. I think that everyone needs some passion, some god to follow. You have yours. It is books."

She said that he was both weak and strong. Strong because he was able to figure out how to survive when he was gone, which must have required both luck and cunning, and strong because he had the sense to desert. To come home. To make it back.

"But you are weak as well. And I recognize the weakness because it comes from the same place as mine. A fear of losing something. I know that you have thought about going to talk to Martens, and that you even imagine taking Katka and bringing her back here. I know this about you because you are moral. And someone who is moral would think that way. But I also know that you don't go because you are afraid of losing Martens' favour. That you think he will take away your bookshop, that he will cut off all money, that you will be completely without a living. And I know that, like me, you love fine things. You like to lie back on your bed above your bookshop in Ekaterinoslav, after making love to the woman, and smoke a cigarette, the woman at your side but already forgotten, and you anticipate going back down to your shop to take up a novel and to lose yourself in it. You are weak because you are selfish. And I accept that."

She paused. Asked him what he saw.

"Beauty. Kindness. Not selfish. No. Very quick with the brain. And with words. I would lose every time. But you don't argue. I am lucky."

She asked if he was still hungry. He said no, he had had enough.

She said, "You have tasted all kinds. This one is Karine, that one is Marta, another is Irena, and then many whose names

I have never heard. Let's not forget your first wife. I am just one more."

He shook his head. He said that all those others were gone. Kaput. Out of his mind.

"I promise to stay with you," she said. "Even if you are crippled, or blind. Until you die. That is my vow."

"And I make you the same promise. I will stay with you. There will be no other. Though I am sure I will die before you."

"Oh, no. Don't."

"So now we are married?" he said.

"We are, in fact."

"May I kiss your hand?" he said.

"Yes. Yes."

Wedding night. It was calm. The small bed they now shared held them easily. And after, while Inna slept, Lehn lit a candle and read a few pages from Gogol, smiling. And then, he too slept.

6.

The Executioner

There was a Ukrainian worker, Andriy, who cleaned the stables on the estate and helped with the horses. Originally from Gulyai-Polye, he now lived with his wife and one child in the village bordering the Martens estate. Since Inna had left, Andriy and Sablin had become closer. Perhaps Sablin now had more time to spend with another, or no one to tie him down anymore, or it might have been the loss he felt, an emptiness. Or perhaps it was their shared dislike of authority. Or their love of horses. Or their common plight — workers on an estate with little pay and no hope of ever owning their own horse, let alone tilling their own land. Andriy was a talker. And a reader. He gave Sablin tracts to read. Newspapers. Books. All about the rights of the worker, the peasant. Sablin tried to read what was offered, but he usually fell asleep and when Andriy asked him about it the next day, he lied and said that it was interesting.

"You never read it," Andriy said.

Sablin agreed. Said that there was no point. "I, Sablin, am going to knock down a powerful man like Martens? Even if I could, I like him. He's good to me."

"Has he beaten you?"

"Not lately."

"Does he pay you what you're worth?"

"What am I worth?"

"Look at you. Strong. Big. The biggest on the estate. Doing all the heavy lifting. Training the horses. How would he replace you?"

"There are others like me. Certainly."

Andriy said that there was no one else like him. He was unique. Did he not know that?

He didn't. He smiled. They were in Sablin's room beside the stable. It was after supper. Andriy wanted him to come to a meeting that evening, in a nearby village. They would take the two bicycles. Return them in the dark. No one would know.

"Martens knows everything," Sablin said.

Andriy left and returned an hour later with the bicycles. "We have Martens's blessing," he said.

"Truly? Where did you say we were going?"

"To the river. To fish. Come."

The air was warm, the sun was setting, grasshoppers jumped, and Andriy had shed his jacket and now his elbows were bare. Such a calmness. Even as Andriy shouted back at him to ride. Faster.

The meeting was a turmoil. Hundreds of people outside, women, men, children. They kept their bicycles close, so as not to lose them. Many spoke. One, whose voice excited the crowd immediately. One of Makhno's people, Andriy said. Sablin did not know who Makhno was. This speaker, though, was interesting. A woman. She excited the crowd by talking about their right to houses, to land, to farms. "It is not theirs. It is yours. Hang the rich. Hang, hang without fail, so the people see, no fewer than one hundred known kulaks, rich men, bloodsuckers. Publish their names. Take from them all the grain."

The crowd cheered like a large animal, swaying, crying out. Sablin was part of the animal. Andriy raised his fist. Sablin imitated him. Andriy grinned and put his arm around Sablin's neck and kissed him on the forehead. "See? See? It is happening."

They cycled home side by side. Andriy lifted his nose, took a deep breath, and said that he smelled something. Change. Definitely. He reached out and took Sablin's hand. They rode like that. It was dark. Half a moon. A perfect night.

That night Andriy did not go back to his village. He slept in Sablin's bed. Andriy talked. His voice was flushed and low and sometimes shaky. He put his hands on Sablin. Confessed that he was full of anger. Always. But when he was at a meeting like the one that night, he lost the anger for a moment, and he felt something new and fresh. "We're still young," he said. "Makhno has an army."

"You have a family," Sablin said.

"Exactly. A son. Who should have what I don't."

It was quiet.

"Do you like this?" Andriy asked.

"I do," Sablin said.

"Good, then."

It was again quiet, save for the movement of the horses in the nearby stalls.

In the morning, looking down from above upon the night that had passed, Sablin thought of Inna. Was glad that she was gone. He went to more meetings. He came to accept that Andriy would join him in his bed. He anticipated it but saw it as temporary. He studied the young woman Elsa and began to talk to her. She allowed this. The world was shifting. Inna had always said that Sablin was smart. She had encouraged his learning. And if learning from books was harder for him than most, she knew that his mind was quick with assessment and deduction. He understood the duplicity of man. He just didn't say anything about it. His father had been gone for years. His mother died when he was seventeen. He had always had Inna, and then she went to live with Lehn, the bookshop owner, and she had Wenig's baby, which Sablin had yet to see or visit. One day soon, he thought.

And then that day came. He was to go to Rosental to pick up little Katka, the baby, and bring her back for Wenig and Irmgard. Elsa would go with him. Elsa was his fiancée. They had been engaged for two months now, which meant that they saw each other on the estate where they both worked, and they talked there occasionally, not often, usually in the afternoon. He had known her for a few years. She was the one who, when he was younger, had touched his head when feeding him break-fast. He had kept his eye on her, and when they had a moment together, she did the talking. He knew this: her own family had no land, no farm, no cows. They rented a house from a man called Lepp. There were seven sisters, no brothers, and because they were very poor, they were all sent out to work for the wealthy landowners. Every Saturday, after being paid, she walked the five miles back to her home and gave the money to her mother, who stored it in a sock beneath her pillow. Her sisters did as she did, though they worked on different farms and different estates. One for Jantz, another for Krueger. She was the only daughter working at the Martens estate. She was the second youngest, and sometimes she seemed spoiled, other times headstrong, and other times haughty. Her father had taught her to read and write, both German and Ukrainian. She had a knack for working with animals, which she preferred to toiling in the kitchen. One day, after a lunch of summer savoury soup and white buns fresh from the oven, she put on rubber boots and pulled up her dress and tramped out to the shed to help Sablin with the horses. If he was surprised to see her, he didn't say. She said a few words and he maybe said one word. She didn't seem fazed by his lack of voice. This surprised him. Just as he had been surprised when, three months later, he stumbled out a proposal for marriage and she said yes, very quickly, and with a smile. Shocking. And he must have looked shocked, because she laughed and said, "Are you sure? Or are you joking?"

He shook his head. He said that he was sure. He saw them riding off from the wedding in one of Martens's painted carriages, carried along by steaming black horses.

◄►

And then came the day when Martens gave Sablin orders to ride to Rosental to pick up his niece Katka — Martens used the word *niece*, and Sablin thought, Why, of course, I am an uncle. During the carriage ride, Elsa told him that Wenig and Irmgard intended to keep the child. This wasn't a Sunday visit.

He didn't believe her. And then, when it became clear that it was true, he said that the child was Wenig's as well and so he had the right.

Elsa said that they could turn around right now and go back to Martens and say that Inna wasn't home. That she was in Ekaterinoslav with the child. Why not?

He shook his head. Even if Martens believed them, he would have them return the following weekend. Or the next day. Until they came back with little Katka.

"She won't know Wenig," Elsa said. "Or Irmgard."

"She's young. She won't remember any of this. Do you recall your life at two?"

Elsa was silent. Her hands were folded on her lap. She wore a dress that she had made for herself that week. He noticed it. Was aware of clothing and footwear and hairstyles, even though he himself was not given to fancy attire. But he saw it on Elsa, and he saw the pleasure on her face when she first showed it to him, outside his little shack at the edge of the estate. Sablin was still landless, even though he was considered an almost-son of Heinrich Martens. He had asked Martens for his own small plot, to own and take care of. He wanted his own horses. A cow. Some chickens. For when he was married. Which was imminent. Martens said that it was impossible to divide up the land. The inheritance would go to the youngest. Who was now Wenig. Those were the rules. But he offered Sablin a small hut, for which he had to pay nothing. It would be his to take care of. Martens said this with such ease that it seemed natural and generous. Sablin took the offer — and dreamed of his own land that led down to the river, land that he would till, and plant and harvest. Elsa hadn't entered his hut yet. That would come.

Elsa's hands were large and strong. She had a solid body. She overwhelmed him with her feelings. Now, on the carriage, rolling past fields of grain and hay, she said that it was a sin what they were doing.

"I don't believe in sin," Sablin said.

"Just because you don't believe in sin doesn't mean it isn't out there, digging around in people's hearts and minds. You don't take a baby from a mother."

"My sister knew this. I told her so."

"I told her so." She was mocking him. "You let him push you around, Sablin. H.H. as well. He has quick hands, all over the women in the house, as if he owned us."

"He's touched you?"

"I don't let him. But he tries to, like Wenig with your sister. H.H. has fat fingers."

"I'll kill him," Sablin said.

"No you won't. For my sake."

Her hands were folded in her lap. On her dress. When a breeze crossed her body, he caught her scent. He didn't say anything. Just kept glancing down at her hands.

They found Inna waiting in the yard with Katka, who was dressed as if going to church. Inna came to them and took Sablin's hands and called him handsome. He'd never thought of himself that way, in fact he didn't see himself in any way, except when others used words to describe him. Which made him shy and self-conscious. He suffered doubt. At that moment, he thought Elsa might be right, tell Martens that Inna was gone, there was no child. But then Inna said that Katka was ready, take her, and she fell to beating Sablin's chest, and so he didn't know if he was to take her or leave her and, in the end, he took her because Inna had allowed it. After beating him, she had disappeared around the house.

On the way home, his chest still felt Inna's fists. Elsa held Katka in her lap and smelled her head and cried and fed her apricots. Katka seemed happy.

He sensed Elsa's disgust. Her shame. Her disappointment.

For a week, she did not talk to him. She worked in the kitchen of the estate, and he knew that she would have knowledge of little Katka, but she said nothing, and he didn't ask.

One Sunday he prepared the carriage for Wenig and Irmgard. They came out of the house, dressed for church, Irmgard holding Katka. Sablin helped Irmgard climb up into the carriage while Wenig held Katka. He was aware of the child. Kept slipping glances her way. The white bonnet. Pressed white dress. White shoes with straps. Babbling. The horses were eager. Pulled at the traces. He talked to them. And then stepped back as Wenig shook the reins and called out.

Elsa came to see him at his hut the following week. She stood outside in her maid's outfit. She looked at him and said that she couldn't marry him. "We are not the same," she said.

He was mute. He wondered if she knew about Andriy.

She said that she had been taught certain things. Don't lie. Don't cheat. Don't steal. And now she had participated in evil, and she felt like she had been dipped in sheep shit.

Sablin was surprised by her language. She had never been vulgar.

She said that he had revealed himself and she didn't like what she saw. "You might claim that you will change, that you will be a better man, that this was one mistake, but people don't change. You won't change."

"You're right. I won't. I just did my job."

Elsa made fists with her big hands. She turned away. After that, he saw her now and then on the estate, but she wouldn't look at him. She must have told the other women working there that the engagement was broken, for now they turned away from him when he passed them by. Sablin didn't understand how her mind worked, other than to know that she would want more than what he had to offer, which was only himself, nothing.

how her mind worked, other than to know that she would want more than what he had to offer, which was only himself, nothing.

Martens called for a meeting with Tolya, the estate manager, and H.H., and Sablin. Sablin didn't understand why he was included, but he went, because Martens had told him to come. Lenin had published a land decree abolishing all estates and property, with no compensation. The peasants were returning from the front, eager to take whatever they could. The day before, three men in a carriage had arrived at Jakob Muss's estate and demanded horses and cows and grain. Muss had waved a revolver and chased them off. But they would return, certainly with more men, and weapons. It was not safe for the women. Martens said that the carriage factory had been stormed. First the workers wanted eight-hour days, then they wanted the factory itself. Production had stopped. He said that the family was going to Kiev for a time. The plan was to stay there for several weeks, until events settled themselves. He would go. And Wenig. Along with the women. He said, "If peasants come, slaughter the cows before giving them up. Give the grain away to neighbours. Burn the house if necessary. Nothing should fall into the hands of those soulless marauders. I trust no one. I pay no attention to insults. I depend on God as my Saviour."

He was putting H.H. in charge, with Tolya as second-in-command, and Sablin as third. "Do you understand?" he asked. Sablin understood. He was to protect the Martens estate, and for that he might be killed.

H.H. was talking now. He said that the peasants had no

idea how to farm, or till, or care for an orchard. "Give a peasant this house and this land and the livestock? They would run it to the ground. No sense of value or morality. If they build a house, it will be of sod, and the window frames would be crooked, if there were window frames at all."

Sablin saw Irmgard slide by silently outside the sitting room, holding Katka, who was coughing. Later, Elsa found Sablin, and for the first time in weeks said some words to him. "Katka is very sick. A high fever. They are going to take her to Kiev, to see a doctor. Irmgard was crying yesterday. And she screamed at Wenig. I took little Katka. She was so hot. Her eyes are milky, and she shakes."

Sablin said that he'd been eyeing Martens's stallion. He didn't want some peasant to get his hands on it.

"You plan to get your hands on it."

"We'll see." He said that the new government had given the villagers the right to take whatever they wanted. Factories. Horses. Cows. Pigs. Grain. Land.

She didn't know. No one had told her anything.

The family left for Kiev, most of the workers were dismissed, Andriy as well, and Sablin missed him, the talks, the agreements, the shared bed. The estate was now quiet, strangely so. Tolya ran off. H.H. raged at his disloyalty. Now they were two. Sablin slept in his hut and worked with the livestock during the day while H.H. kept to the house. They did not speak, except for one time when H.H. found Sablin in the stable and asked if Sablin wanted to sleep in the big house where it was safer.

Sablin said that he preferred his hut. It was familiar.

H.H. nodded. Rolled a cigarette and lit it. Said he was grateful that Sablin hadn't run off like Tolya.

"Where would I go?" Sablin said.

"True. But still. My father sees it. I see it. Your loyalty."

Sablin was uneasy. It was difficult to know what H.H. truly believed in, other than the guarding of his possessions.

"Do you need a gun?" H.H. asked.

Sablin shook his head.

"A knife? A sabre?"

Nothing.

Chickens were stolen one night, so now Sablin slept in the barn, comforted by the movements of the cows and horses.

A week later news came that Katka had died.

Early the following day he prepared the stallion and told H.H. he would be back the next day, as he didn't want to ride at night. H.H. protested. Sablin ignored him. Left him standing by the gate that opened onto the path that led to the large house. He was holding his rifle.

On the road, he passed wagons piled high with furniture and goods, pulled by fine horses, usually a man holding the traces, a woman beside him, children piled on top of the furniture, sometimes just men, cheering. Villagers coming home from looting. It was obvious by their manner, and their dress. They looked poor. A manor on fire in the distance. Smoke lifting. Clear sky. Almost white in the brilliant sun. No one stopped him. No one asked him for his horse. He should have taken the older grey, not this beauty. Before crossing the river to Rosental, he saw a cloud of dust lifting, and heard the battering hooves before he saw the men. He went off the road into a shelter of trees and watched the gang gallop by, very close, a wild assortment, some dressed in tatters, one in a black suit as if going to church, another in a long black cape, swinging a sabre. All rode good horses, certainly stolen.

He arrived at Rosental at dusk, where he found Inna and

Lehn eating in the kitchen. Inna stood when she saw him and put her hand to her mouth. He told her. And she wailed. And wailed. Lehn held her but was pushed away. Sablin walked outside. Put his horse in the stable and found some grain and fed him and washed him and said how strong he was, and handsome, and in the morning they would ride again but for now he would eat and drink and then sleep. He talked about how tall he was, and the beauty of his short mane, such a rich-looking beast, and Sablin told him again how handsome he was, and the words went in circles and he repeated himself, but the horse didn't mind. Sablin put his head against the beast's chest and heard the heart pumping and he thought of hearts in general, and then of hearts more carefully, Inna's, and Elsa's, and then Katka's little heart, and he pushed aside that thought and lay down in the straw beside the horse and fell asleep. And woke to Inna's voice telling him to come inside.

"Come."

He followed her, and she set a plate of corn and beef and potatoes before him. He ate quickly, with great hunger. She gave him more. She asked him about Katka, had he seen anything of her before the family left, and he confessed that he hadn't, though Elsa had, and seeing Inna's eyes, he said that Elsa had held Katka before the family left for Kiev. Had spent the day with her, and at that point Katka had been clear-eyed, and not too sick, though she had cried out for her real mother, and so she still remembered Inna.

"Oh, oh," Inna said. "I know you're lying, but okay."

Inna said that the child had been dead to her when she was taken. But there had always been the hope that she was happy, and growing, and well cared for. And that one day she might see her again, even if it was years from now. "A child remembers. In here." And she pressed her hand to her chest.

She asked after Elsa. How was she?

Sablin said that she was gone. Everyone was gone. Only H.H. was left.

"And your wedding?"

"Perhaps," Sablin said. "After."

Inna said that Johann Lepp's father had been shot by bandits, and the next day Johann married Ana Hamm in Hochfeld #2.

"I'll tell Elsa that," Sablin said.

Inna's cheeks were red and chapped. Her eyes dark. Hands raw. Lehn entered and put a hand on Inna's head.

Inna looked at him, and then told Sablin that they were married now, she and Lehn.

Sablin said, "Good. That's good for you."

"A small wedding," Inna said. "Just the two of us." Then she said, "You don't need a church."

"I'll mention that to Elsa as well. Though she believes in church."

He was talking nonsense, something he never did, but why would Inna need to know anything about his failures. He said, "Martens has all this livestock, and the horses, and I'm not sure he'll have it much longer."

"Herman Koop is praying and waiting for the Germans to show up," Inna said.

"Martens as well," Sablin said.

Lehn was brewing something hot. He gave a cup to Sablin. It tasted of hawthorn.

The following day, riding back to the estate, he was chased

by a band of peasants out on the open road. His horse was fast
and strong, and he easily outran the band, who didn't have
much skill. Mastering horses was new to them. Still, he was
wary now, and each time he saw dust in the distance, he sought
out a grove of trees in which to hide. The men who passed by
on the road carried pitchforks and guns and sabres and they
rode carelessly, whipping the horses. Sablin felt great pity for
the animals.

H.H. met him in the barn and announced that Klassen
and his family had been shot. The estate manager as well. And
Huss and his sons. The women had been spared. And news
had come from Tokmak that old Sudermann from Apanlee
and Heinrich Neufeld had been shot. Gutsbesitzer Wiens had
been shot to death as well. His estate burned. H.H. said it was
the Bolsheviks working up the anger of the peasants. "They are
wild animals. They shoot you and then take the furniture from
your house. And the blankets. And dishes." He said that he had
fired on a group of three men the night before. Scared them off.

Sablin listened. He wiped down the stallion. Let him out
to pasture.

Now that the workers were gone, H.H. was cooking. They
ate together in the manor dining room, at opposite ends of
the long table. H.H. talked while Sablin listened. More news
of killings and rapes.

"I am not married," H.H. said. "This is the way of the Lord.
So be it. But if I were a married man, and anyone touched my
wife, I would shoot them in the head." His fat fingers held his
fork and knife daintily, as if he were royalty. It had always been
so, H.H. tiptoeing his way through the meal like a young girl
in a meadow.

The day before he was killed, H.H. tried to ride one of his

father's young stallions, who hadn't been broken properly, and hated the rope, and any object on its back. Sablin captured it, roped it, tied it up so that H.H. could climb on board, and then loosed the rope. H.H. was thrown immediately. He told Sablin to have a go. Sablin shook his head. "If I say go, you go," H.H. said.

Sablin talked to the trembling horse. Touched its withers, mane, forelock. All was allowed. Ran a rope along the neck and across its short topline. Down towards the barrel. The horse shivered. Sablin looked into the horse's eyes. He turned and said that the horse needed time. Tomorrow morning he would try. Now was too early. "He needs to rest. To drink. To eat."

H.H. grunted and walked away.

At dawn Sablin woke to a clatter of horses, and shouts, the barking of a dog, a squeal like a pig slaughtered, gibberish, more great shouts. He dressed quickly and ran from the stable to the yard, where twenty men gathered in a circle, and at the centre of that circle was H.H. on his knees, a rope around his neck. His face was beaten. His eyes had swelled. He could not see. He reached out with his hands and groped and begged. The men kicked at him. He fell onto his chest.

Sablin saw Tolya at the front, he appeared to be giving directions. They dragged H.H. to the orchard. One of the men was testing the branches of the trees, and like an arborist in his element he announced them too short and too weak. "To the barn," Tolya cried, and they dragged H.H. into the stable, where the horses paced nervously, and the calves skittered into a corner and raised their noses. One man threw the rope over a beam and many men pulled H.H. up so that his feet were off the ground. His hands reached for his neck. His legs kicked for a long time, as if he were a puppet being toyed with by a child. The thrashing stopped. He had wet himself. A coward, someone said. Sablin was noticed at the back of the group and was caught and thrown beneath the feet of the dead man. A rope was put around his neck. He was kicked in the chest. And then Tolya stepped forward and released the rope and lifted Sablin to his feet, looked into Sablin's eyes, kissed him on the mouth, and said that this was a brother.

The sun rose. The manor was turned upside down. Furniture was hauled out to the yard and placed in carriages. The heavy dining room table was carried by eight men. The Kroeger clock as well, and as it was placed in a wagon, it tolled the hour and the men fell back, afraid at first, and then laughing and clapping each other. One man pulled out his rifle and shot at it till the tolling stopped. More cheering. When the pillaging was complete, Tolya said to burn the manor down. A calf was slaughtered and hung from an iron rod and roasted at the edge of the great fire. It was too hot to approach, and in the end the meat was charred and blackened and inedible. And was eaten. Sablin watched in amazement. He found Tolya and said, head bowed, "Not the barn. Not the horses and cows."

Tolya grinned. "Okay. For you, Sablin, no barn burning."

They left at midday, with the house still burning, smoke lifting high into a bright sky. They took fresh horses. Tolya took Martens's stallion. Sablin was left with the two grey geldings. "A gift for you," Tolya said.

"Join us," Tolya said. "It is your right. You have nothing. They have everything."

Sablin shook his head. He was confused. He understood, and he didn't understand.

And then they were gone. And it was completely quiet save for the occasional pop from one of the large oak beams still burning in the sitting room. Beams that smouldered over the following week.

He felt great sadness for the horses that were lost. About H.H. he felt a slight surprise at the ease with which a man could die. Little pity. And some bewilderment at Tolya's involvement, the two faces of the man, the matter-of-fact betrayal, killing the son of the man for whom he had worked so many years. It was a mystery, but then not such a mystery. He imagined doing the same to Wenig, holding in a poisonous part of his heart a great hatred for the man. And why not? A decree had been called down from on high, and the rules had been rewritten. What had been right, was now wrong. And what was wrong, was now right. And he was right, and Martens was wrong. Though Martens, should he return, would still see himself as someone who had been wronged.

He fed the livestock, gathered eggs, salvaged what he could from the manor — some dishes, drinking glasses, a few books from the library, a single blanket that smelled of smoke, Mrs. Martens's clothes from a still-standing wardrobe, warped kitchenware, a colander. The root cellar beneath the kitchen was untouched. There were preserves, and smoked ham, and wheat that had been ground, and milk still in pitchers. He cooked in his hut. Ate at a small table. Thought he might be waiting for something, but what that was he could not say. He imagined that the land was now his. And his hut was his. And the barns and stable and sheep and the water from the well and the two greys with their sore fetlocks, the chickens, the milk cows, the hogs. He fed the animals, milked the cows twice a day, kept the barns clean, and realized that the crops were ready for harvest. It was late. Though if he were attacked again, none of this was his. He was not a landowner, nor did he have anything of value. Go ahead, take it. Still, he became attached to the idea of ownership, and in the morning, early, he walked around the burned-down manor, and he walked out towards his fields, and he ran his hands through his grain, and he felt a certain pleasure in what might be. Perhaps Martens was dead as well. Killed by typhoid. And Wenig, shot by Bolsheviks. He cleaned H.H.'s rifle and made sure he had ammunition. He would protect this place from marauders. It was now his to defend.

Earlier, a day after the attack, he had cut down H.H. and loaded him onto a wagon and hitched the wagon to the geldings and rode to the church in Village #3, where he handed H.H. to Pastor Krahn, the lay minister. A crowd gathered. Murmurings. Questions. He had no answers. They came, they killed, they left. Why had he survived? He shrugged. He was lucky. He did not speak of Tolya. Someone must have notified Martens, because a telegram was delivered that told Sablin to stay put and take care of whatever remained.

And then, for reasons that Sablin did not understand, the countryside went quiet, and the peasants were no longer seen, and the roads were now full of German soldiers, on horseback, in carriages, marching, filling up the land. They asked for lodging and food and were welcomed by those in the colonies. And now the shoe was on the other foot, and anyone with revolutionary leanings or Red Guard connections was arrested: Friesen and his sons, Neufeld, Braun from Lichtenau — all in prison. Those Ukrainian villagers who had participated in the robberies and pillaging were hunted down and shot. The more pacifist landowners said that vengeance was not theirs to mete out, it was God's, though they were grateful for the presence of the Germans.

Wenig and Martens returned without their wives to the estate. Martens kissed Sablin on the mouth, something new. Sablin gave the hut to them and moved back into the stable. Martens asked how H.H. had died. Sablin told him. Martens wept at the sight of the rubble, and then announced that a new house would be built. Tolya was hunted. Wenig heard that he had fled to Alexandrovsk. He left one day on one of the greys, and returned a week later riding the stallion, the grey in tow. He did not speak of what had taken place, except to say that Tolya would no longer be needing the horse. They ate, the three of them, in the summer kitchen. Sablin had been designated the cook, and he made many pots of butter soup, until Elsa's sister, Elizabeth, arrived to help. She was younger than Elsa, but more brazen, and she told Sablin right off that Elsa was now married to a young Mennonite man from her village. She was with child.

How quickly love and loyalty shifted. Elsa was like Tolya, twisting with the winds. Even when Martens had beat him, Sablin had accepted the whip as a requirement of employment. A form of affection. A creed to be followed. I might beat you, but I will also give you food and shelter. Sablin thought that this might be love. Certainly, Elsa did not love him as Martens did. Though Sablin would not have given up his life for the man. To what end? Would Martens do the same for Sablin? He doubted it. His fantasy had gone away. He was now no longer the owner of the estate, anticipating the harvest. Such short-lived pleasure. He often saw and heard Wenig and his father whispering, their heads together, faces turned to the ground as if a secret lay in the dirt at their feet. They were having difficulty finding workers to harvest the grain. In the end they found some Mennonite boys to whom Martens offered extra wages.

Wenig didn't work, he was an overseer, and he appeared to also want to oversee Elizabeth, the young cook, and he took to trapping her out in the yard, by the root cellar. Elizabeth always bowed her head when Wenig spoke to her.

Sablin asked Elizabeth if Wenig had touched her.

"Not yet."

"Be careful. His hands are dirty."

She looked at him. She said that Wenig was rich and she was poor. "Like you, Sablin. And why would Wenig be interested in me?"

"You don't know him," Sablin said. "If he touches you, tell me." He turned away.

Martens was suddenly older. He walked with a limp. His hands shook. All day, in Sablin's hut, he drew up plans for the new manor, and then presented the most recent drawing at supper, this one would have fifty rooms and indoor toilets for all, even the workers. Wenig humoured him, Sablin said nothing. Wenig was keen to join the local Selbstschutz, a military group made of men from various villages, armed and trained by the Germans.

Martens said that it was foolishness. It could only come to grief.

Wenig regarded him as if he was a doddering fool. "Who will stop them, if not us?"

"First the peasants, then the Reds. Where will it stop? Death begets death." Martens banged the small table. The soup jumped. The silverware rattled.

One day they travelled, the three men, to Ohrloff, where there was a festival for the German soldiers. Villagers had come from various parts and now numbered two thousand. A military band played. There was a display of gymnastics put on by a local Selbstschutz. Some marching and an exhibition of revolvers and rifles. Sausage sandwiches were served along with beer, and ice cream and raspberries were sold. Wenig flirted with a shy young woman, held a rifle briefly, and talked with the Germans. Sablin watched and drank beer. Martens sat on a wooden chair at the edge of a meadow and spoke with a circle of men his age.

A German soldier strolled by and said something to Sablin. He looked up. The soldier held a camera, and he was pointing at it and then at Sablin. "Can I?" he asked. "Take your photo?"

Sablin looked around, surprised. Then he said yes.

The German was older, perhaps in his thirties. His uniform was neat and clean, and his hair was longer, and the curls fell behind his ears. His boots shone. He took several photographs. "Lift your chin," he called to Sablin, and Sablin obeyed. Children gathered. The German took photos of the children, gave them money for dessert, and ran them off. "They remind me of my own children," he said. He had a daughter and a son. Back in Danzig. The Kaiser allowed soldiers to carry cameras, to record the war, as long as it didn't interfere with the fighting. He said that he preferred the camera to the gun. His name was Günter Birr. He sat down beside Sablin and began to talk about the beauty of Ukraine, and the beauty of the women. "Though Germany did not invade because the women have beautiful eyes," he said. "We came for the bread." He laughed.

He was soft, not hard. He wanted details of Sablin's life. Sablin said that he was with Martens, who owned a carriage factory. Birr got excited and said that the German settler carriages were the strongest and gave the best ride. "What a machine," he said. And then Sablin began to talk about the horses he cared for, in particular the stallion, and then the burning of the manor, and the shooting of the grandfather clock. He left out many details, such as the hanging.

Birr said that he would come to the estate, as it was his job to record both the ugly and the beautiful. He asked for directions. And then he said goodbye.

Over the next days Sablin kept lifting his head at the slightest sound of hooves, or movement out on the road, as if Birr's arrival was imminent. He did not come, and so Sablin forgot him. Though there were moments when images arrived: his hair curling behind his ears, the familiar tones in his German, the gentleness of his manner. One day, in the stable where Sablin was paring one of the grey's hooves, Wenig said that if Sablin had taken initiative and bedded Elsa, then he wouldn't have lost her to some useless Mennonite boy. "Elizabeth told me that she's now married and pregnant. Some women, you just have to look at them and they're with child."

Sablin stood. He was holding the knife used to cut the hooves. He said, "If you touch Elizabeth, if you lay a hand on her, I will first beat your head in, and then I will kill you."

Wenig's mouth moved, but no words came. He sputtered some more, and then left the stable.

Sablin expected that Wenig would run to tell his father, but at supper no words were spoken about the stable incident. Elizabeth served, and when she passed by Wenig, she touched his shoulder, just a small graze, and when this happened, Wenig shrugged her away and looked at Sablin. Who was watching. Martens was studying the potatoes on his spoon, oblivious.

Wenig announced that he had joined the Selbstschutz of a nearby colony and that he would be training with them early each morning for three hours. He would use his father's stallion.

"You will be going nowhere," Martens said. "There will be no more soldiers in my family. There will be no more killing."

Wenig said that he was old enough to choose for himself. He would go.

The rest of the meal was eaten in silence. The clink of the dinnerware, the sound of Wenig chewing. The heavy sighs from Martens.

Wenig left early the following morning. He asked Sablin to prepare the stallion with the Whitman saddle and Sablin obeyed, smelling the leather of the saddle, and whispering in the horse's ear.

All that day Martens tottered like a mendicant about the estate, surveying the remains of the manor, heading out to the orchards. Sablin saw him standing for the longest time, staring out over the stubbled fields that sloped towards the creek. He was crying. He had always worn the best of clothes and so it still was. His boots shone, his jacket had a tail, and he wore the fedora that, as he liked to tell the story, he had purchased from a *Kurzwaren* in Vienna when he had travelled there with his niece Katka years earlier.

That evening, after Wenig had returned from military exercises and was talking headlong about the militia and the Germans who were training them, and the guns and the power of the guns, Martens shushed him and said that he was returning to Kiev. His family was there. He would go by train. "There is nothing left here." Wenig protested. Martens held up a hand and said, "Enough. I have decided."

Sablin took him to the train station the following morning. Martens was quiet. As was Sablin. The creak of the traces, the breathing of the horses, the smell of dust from the harvest, the sun rising red. And then Martens spoke. He said that the Lord permitted so much that could not be understood. He talked about Job, and what was taken from him. He did not claim to be Job, however. He had done wrong. He was a sinner. He said that his greatest wrong was taking little Katka from her mother. From Inna. It had been Annalee's plan, and Wenig's. And he had gone along with it like a sheep being led about in the night. He said that there was nothing to be done now. "The punishment has come. Look at me. No longer the leader in my own family. Homeless. My factory taken. My wagons, painted with beautiful flowers, are now used to carry machine guns. I am ashamed for who man is. What we've become." He went silent. Sablin did not answer. He had nothing to say. He felt little for the man, who still seemed proud even as he cried about his shame.

Martens said that what was left was now Wenig's to care for. To keep or to lose. He thanked Sablin for his loyalty. He did not offer anything, no horse, no land, no proceeds from the grain, just thanked him.

The plan had been that Martens would ride in a first-class carriage, but the German soldiers had commandeered all the seats, and so he settled on second class, but that too was overbooked. The station was occupied by Austrian soldiers. The crowds were overwhelming. A place was found finally in a cattle car with no seats. Martens considered waiting for another train, and then climbed on with Sablin's assistance. "This is what it has come to," he said. "Look at me."

Elizabeth had been dismissed, and so Sablin spent his days alone. Some nights Wenig did not return, and then one day Wenig announced that he would be billeted at a companion's house in a nearby village. The training was important, and the attacks on the villages were increasing, even with the presence of the Germans. And so Sablin was by himself, and though he was not lonely, he realized that there was nothing left for him on this place, but then what to do, where to go, where was there a place for him? To ease the restlessness he spent his days mending saddles, repairing traces, tending the livestock. He churned butter. For whom, he did not know, though he thought if he did leave, he would tell Elizabeth and Elsa and the sisters to come and take what was left. They had earned it. At night sometimes he heard guns, and horses running, but no bandits came to the estate, perhaps because the house was no more, and it looked abandoned.

One day Birr arrived. He came alone. Sablin heard him before he saw him and thought, Here are bandits. But it was only Birr, who asked if there was room for one soldier and two horses.

They ate in the summer kitchen, where Sablin built a fire, as it was getting cooler now. He cooked his usual, butter soup. He offered Birr the hut where Wenig had been sleeping, but Birr said he would sleep where Sablin slept. In the barn. And once again Sablin noted how grand Birr was with his gestures, and his storytelling, and his heart. No resentments. Not a worry. Photographs of his children and his wife and his small house in Danzig. The camera at hand. He took photographs of the land, the ruins of the manor, the stable, the outbuildings, the workers' quarters, the orchards, the remaining horses, Sablin with the horses, Sablin alone. Many photos of Sablin, until Sablin said, Enough. He was embarrassed.

Birr showed Sablin how to operate the camera, so that now Sablin was taking photos of Birr. Birr set up a darkroom in the root cellar and developed the film there, among the smoked pork and the cheese and butter. Sablin watched, and listened, learned quickly. Birr had two cameras, both Ango high speed, German made. Birr liked to describe everything for Sablin, how to adjust the shutter for desired speed, how to unfold the camera and focus on the ground glass, the tension on the spring, the length of the curtain slit, the plates that held the film.

One evening, at dusk, Birr dressed Sablin in a pair of his boots, and a German uniform, and bandoliers with a pistol, and a rifle. Oiled his hair for him and combed it back so that Sablin's long forehead was prominent. And his nose. Birr said that he loved Sablin's jaw. He touched it.

He kissed Sablin that night, after they drank the port that Birr pulled from his saddlebag. Birr tasted of dried fruit and the burn of Aleikum cigarettes. They shared the room alongside the horses who, at night, shuffled and lifted their heads and listened to the two men. Beautiful boy. Birr said this. And Sablin began to talk. He told stories of his mother. He spoke in a halting German, with Russian words worked in out of necessity. Birr listened. Lying beside each other, they held hands. He had felt close to Inna in this manner. He talked about missing her. About Katka, the child. Who was dead.

In the morning he rose early to milk the cows while Birr slept. Then he returned to the bed with warm milk in a clay cup. Birr drank. Dipped his fingers in the milk and slid them into Sablin's mouth.

Birr had no politics. When Sablin talked about the peasants who attacked the estates, and how he understood them, Birr said that only monkeys would act like that, and then he angled Sablin's jaw so that the light caught him a certain way. "Perfect," he said.

Birr left after two weeks. The German army was with-drawing. Horses would be auctioned. This being so, he gave

Sablin his brown mare, and some Salem cigarettes, and one of his Ango cameras and three plates, along with solutions and papers for developing.

And so it was that Sablin came to know photography.

◧

On a cold day in late December, Wenig Martens was killed by the Machnovtze along with a German officer during the defence of a village in the Chortitza colony. Sablin, because Martens had requested this of him, attended the funeral. After the sermon, based on Job 7:1 — "Do not mortals have hard service on earth? Are not their days like those of hired labourers?" — the procession passed in a very military manner between two columns of men on horseback, and at the cemetery Wenig's unit sang "Ich hatt' einen Kameraden." The crowd numbered close to one thousand and Sablin was lost within the mass of people. He felt nothing for Wenig, though he did feel a slight pain for Martens, who had now lost his three sons and his granddaughter. At the cemetery he slipped close to the burial and took a photograph of the young men who carried the casket. He developed the photograph and had it delivered to the Martens family in Kiev. He had been practising at the estate with the camera, taking photographs of the horses, and the land around, but this was the first time he had photographed people, and though at first his hands were shaking, and he believed someone might stop him, he discovered that the camera was respected, and it was like a shield, and he was not seen as a poor peasant boy, but as a young man who wielded a certain power. People liked the idea of being seen, of being held in one place in a certain space. It was to his benefit that people were generally self-centred.

It was at the funeral that he heard the Red Army was requiring young men his age to register for the military. Horses were being requisitioned again. Grain. Cows. He had no fixed ideas about the world, other than that everyone had an opinion about right and wrong, and that each army was convinced that it had the greatest moral reason for fighting. Inna had once laughingly described him as a tumbleweed because he bounced with the wind, back and forth, with no real direction. Or maybe he just wanted people to see him in that way, she said. "I think you fool people with your softness, your compliance." When she said this, he looked at her and said that the world was not that complicated. People wanted things, and they took them. Even those who claimed it wasn't so. He said that he was no different.

Through Christmas and into the new year he lived alone, taking care of the few remaining animals. He had so far avoided registering for the army. He would not make himself known. Early in the new year Elizabeth reappeared. She asked Sablin if she could work on the estate, for him, for Martens. She would do anything he asked. She didn't have to be paid, she simply needed a place to stay and eat.

"Your family?" Sablin asked.

Her father and mother had been killed by bandits. She turned away and said in a whisper that she had done what was necessary to survive. And now she was here. "Will you have me?"

She slept in the hut, Sablin remained in the stable. He was Ukrainian, and she was Mennonite. They spoke different languages, had different religions, if he believed in anything at all. He was very poor. She was not so poor. Even though her family had very little, he believed that she saw him as lowly, certainly lower than her. Still, there was an attachment. She was Elsa's sister. But more of a talker. She was always asking him what he was thinking and had a way of prying information from him, through misdirection, or softness, laughter.

After supper one evening he told her about taking Katka from her mother. She listened and then asked him, "If you could turn back the clock, would you do it again?"

"A dumb question."

"No, it's a simple question. What have you learned?"

He said no, he wouldn't do it again.

"So, you are different."

"Elsa said that I would never change," he said.

"Elsa is very strict, both with herself and others. I love her, but I wouldn't want to be her husband, or her child." She said that Elsa was the kind of person who thought she could wish bad things away.

He realized that Elizabeth accepted what came to her, and rather than change it, she moved around it. She was like a slow-moving river that found the path to the sea. With no pride. Just practicality and love and joy. He was happy to have someone help with the cooking, the laundry, and the milking, and churning of cheese and butter. She said one evening, as they ate across from each other, that come spring she would plant a garden. He realized that she planned to settle in. And this pleased him in a different way than the discovered pleasure with Andriy and Birr. The relationship with Elizabeth was easy, with no physical expectations, and because there were no expectations, he began to notice her, and to trust her, and he liked her voice as she talked to him as they ate, and he liked her hands with the short bitten nails, and her affection for the natural world. She was good with the milk cow, and with the sheep, and this made her attractive. They survived on what the estate had to offer — they had grain that Sablin took to the mill, and milk, and eggs, and butter, and there were canned vegetables and fruit in the root cellar from the previous year. If necessary, they could slaughter a pig.

One night he talked about Andriy and his vision for the world. His love of Makhno and the anarchists. She said that Makhno was evil. He had killed her parents. When he entered villages with his black guards, they slaughtered the children and beheaded them and left their heads in flowerpots on the sills.

"You saw him kill your parents?"

"I didn't see it, but Buhler the neighbour said it was him."

He said that rumour had Makhno everywhere at once. He was in Tokmak the same night he was in Alexandrov. Here there everywhere. Which meant that he had become bigger than life. His army was growing, and everyone wanted to fight with him, for Makhno would save the peasant.

"Do you want to be saved?" she asked.

"This is how you see me? A peasant."

"You are."

"As are you."

"I don't think so."

"What are you, if not that?"

"I am not you. You are not me."

"Did your family own land?"

She shook her head.

"They are taking the land. From Martens, from Bergmann, from all the owners. It isn't theirs to have. It is for all of us."

She said that all men smelled the same, no matter their beliefs. They were full of lust and violence. Heads full of cud.

He was quiet. Did not disagree.

◄●►

In April, when the earth was warmer, they planted a garden. He took seed potatoes from the cellar, and they dug ten rows and buried 250 potatoes and covered them with earth. Elizabeth had started tomato seeds earlier in March, and come May they set the new plants in the earth, kneeling side by side on the ground. Carrots and beets and beans, seeds discovered in one of the huts set near the stable. Sablin marvelled at Martens and how prepared he had been for the spring planting. One morning they found the chickens scratching through the garden, eating the seeds, and so that day he built a fence around their small patch to keep the chickens out. Down near the apple orchard there were several hives of bees. At the first sign of warmth Elizabeth had removed the covering on the hives and now the bees were roaming, looking for food. Everything was new to him, and there were times when Elizabeth had to teach him, and he asked her where she had learned about gardening and bees and plants. From her father and mother. Of course. He said that he knew about horses and livestock. She would be in charge of the garden.

Their existence was at once intimate and distant. He was aware of her as they kneeled side by side in the garden, and as they ate across from each other, or when she said she would be bathing that evening. He disappeared then and left her to herself, reappearing to find her clean, her hair shining, the ends wet, dressed in one of Mrs. Martens's dresses that had been salvaged from the manor house. She did laundry and hung it up on ropes that he had strung between two trees. Gone was the girl who had innocently flirted with Wenig as she served him at the dinner table. She was older now. She seemed sadder, though she still walked with a light step, and took great pleasure in pointing out to him the seedlings pushing from the earth. These are carrots. These beets. When they talked, usually over meals that she had prepared, she did most of the talking, though sometimes his tongue was looser, and he forgot himself.

One evening, after cleaning his hands with the heated water she had boiled for him, he ate the food she offered. He had found a shirt without holes, and boots that had survived the fire. They were Martens's boots, slightly small for him, but they were boots, and made of leather.

He said that one time he had gone to a meeting with Andriy where anarchists spoke. Everything made sense. The speaker, a woman, was powerful. Her words were clear, and the people had cheered her like a god.

She said that it was a sin to compare a person to God.

He said that he did not believe in sin.

"And God?" she asked.

"There is no god," he said. "Martens, Schroeder, they all believe in god. God is a handy excuse for doing evil."

She laughed and this made him angry. He said that freedom was no laughing matter.

"You are so serious, Sablin," she said. "You will die from crying. What do you want?"

"A horse. A stable. A small piece of land to plant tomatoes and vegetables. To be left alone. That is all."

"That is a lot."

Sometimes, at night, he got up to check the yard, and to walk past her hut. The door was closed. It was dark. He put his ear to the door, heard nothing. In the morning she appeared, dressed, still alive, and he was relieved.

They were still a target for the roaming armies. Troops arrived, one time a Red Army company in retreat, another time a motley group who claimed to be Denikinist and who threatened to shoot him, or to run a sabre through him, though these threats turned out to be idle, mere joking, said with a wry smile and withdrawn after an offering of food and the possibility of a photo shoot. The camera continued to be a curiosity, though he was running out of paper and solution. Elizabeth hid when the armies came, though once or twice she was almost too late, and nearly seen. She hid in the root cellar. Sablin suggested she cut her hair and dress in pants so that she would look like a boy. It would be safer. She agreed, though the loss of her hair saddened her. When loosed from her braids, it hung to her knees, and it was thick and wavy, and hard to cut. He used a knife that he had sharpened, and the sound of the knife going through the hair made her cry out. However, she was not completely vain, and she said that her head felt lighter. By June the back and forth of the various armies became more frequent. With each group, Sablin listened to their speeches and nodded his head at everything that was said. He spoke Russian, Ukrainian, and German with the various groups, though mostly Ukrainian. Always, with each visit, he trembled, not at the thought of being shot but of contracting typhus, which was raging throughout the country. Inevitably, horses were exchanged, so that by the fourth visit of some nomadic company all he had to offer was two nags who had been sorely mistreated. He kept the stallion in a separate stable, hoping that no one would discover him. And no one had yet.

When bands of riders appeared, sometimes fifteen, other times thirty, and entered the yards of the estate, it was first necessary for Sablin to explain that he and Elizabeth were simply peasants, not owners of the estate, and that the owners had left for Kiev. Inevitably, there were questions: do you have money, gold, food, grain, chickens, horses?

Sablin answered that there were only small amounts of food, some bread, some flour, a few eggs. And so it was expected that food would be prepared, and the horses would be stabled and fed and that beds would be provided. Plunder the plunderers, this was the motto. Elizabeth was young enough and slim enough to pass for a young boy. It was important that she not speak, and whenever she was addressed, Sablin would speak for her. If necessary he would explain that Elizabeth was mute. The men slept in the yard, and at night they burned fires.

Elizabeth saw each successive band of men as no different from the previous. Sablin, however, knew them and their designations. These were Bolsheviks. These were anarchists, Makhno's men. These were White Russians. These were Cossacks. These were green, these white, these red, these black. To Elizabeth, it meant nothing. All were the same. Sometimes the same group of men would return to the estate, running back to where they had come from, being chased by another group that had also spent time at the estate. Elizabeth thought that everything that was unholy and stupid about the world and about men had now come to pass.

And then there were two weeks of nothing. Just quiet. They believed that the worst had passed.

On a Sunday morning a group of riders appeared in a great clatter. All had long hair and black capes, and each had a pair of large pistols in his belt. Some wore bell-bottom trousers and gold bracelets. There were wagons with cannons and large guns, and black flags hoisted above those wagons. These men sat on their horses and looked down at Sablin, who was standing in the yard. Elizabeth was near the orchard, hanging laundry, and she had paused, a sheet in her arms. A rider on a tall white horse came forward. A woman. A *kubanka* sat on her head at a tilt. She asked Sablin if he was a landowner. Sablin shook his head.

"I work for Martens, the owner," he said.

The woman said that he was now free. No longer any need to work for the *pomeshchik*.

She dismounted and approached Elizabeth and asked, "Why are you hiding?"

Elizabeth was shaking. She did not speak.

"Do you have food?" the woman asked.

"A little," Sablin said.

"Then we will eat," the woman said, and she turned away.

They ate outside, by the summer kitchen. Sablin killed a chicken and plucked it and Elizabeth made a soup. She baked buns. When the food was ready, the woman said that Sablin and Elizabeth should eat first. He took a little soup, she a bun, and they sat at a wooden table set up on the grass. When Sablin spooned up some soup, and sipped at it, he was aware of the woman watching, and the men behind.

"My name is Marusya. Yours?"

Sablin gave his name.

Marusya repeated it. "And the boy's?"

Sablin said that the boy was called Ens.

"Does he speak?" Marusya asked.

"Not much."

Marusya laughed. "Thank you for the food, Ens," she said. And then she picked up a bun, and she tore it in half, and she ate. She took some soup, and she ate that. And only when she was finished, and had lighted her cigarette, did her men eat.

She came to Sablin later, while her men were drinking by the fire, and she began to talk. Like Andriy she had many answers, and much temerity. She said that the whole of the Dnieper valley, and most of Ukraine, was open to change. Now was the time. She did not believe in telling the peasant what was good for them. "It's simple. Factories to the workers, land to the peasants. The Bolsheviks promise this as well, but they've failed. Completely. What I promise is freedom from the state. Freedom from slave labour. No more oppression. For example, I could say to you, Sablin, that you should join us as we destroy the *pomeshchik*. But I won't force you. It is your choice. Still, whether you join us or not, we will destroy." She took a drink from her tin cup. The crooked edge of her hair above her eyebrows, and the slash of her mouth. She smoked. And talked some more, as if Sablin was a potential convert and she was the preacher. She said that Makhno was someone who thought as she did, though he was too fond of believing the peasant, who was as capable of deceit as the landowner. "Give the peasant land, and they become jealous and protective. It is in our nature, and it is my goal to erase that nature." She said that she and Makhno were like a broom that swept away the dirt of the *pomeshchik,* and if the small peasant landowner, the kulak, got caught up in that cleaning, so be it. The world was full of litter, and she was the cleaner. Those who owned land, a beautiful horse, a cow, a plough, a pig, an orchard, those people would be shot. She kept repeating that the workers and peasants must take what was theirs, which was everything of value, and anything that served their own interests. She was fascinated by vegetable gardens. She had seen his garden, which was flourishing, she said. She admired that. Her chance would come. Again about Makhno. He had strong eyes. A piercing gaze. It was clear from his speeches, which went on and on, that he loved the peasants. Not so much the individual peasant but the idea of the peasant, for whom he was fighting, whose freedom he wanted to deliver. He incited crowds with words that spun out and floated over their heads. Bat'ko Makhno was loved. More than Marusya. She used her own name, Marusya. "More than Marusya." But that was fine. "We both have our morals," she said. "There was a congress in the village of Sentovo. Makhno had organized it to entrap and execute the guerrilla Grigoryev. A man of pogroms, a killer of Jews. For no reason, just because they were Jews. Grigoryev had killed two thousand Jews in Elizavetgrad several weeks before the congress. He was a chameleon, someone who latched himself to whatever was nearest at hand. Petliura, Bolshevism, then Petliura again, and then Denikin. At the congress, Grigoryev spoke first. He proclaimed that allies were needed to eliminate the Bolsheviks. Sleeping with one enemy was essential to destroy the other enemy. Makhno followed with his own speech. He called Grigoryev's plan criminal. He accused him of anti-Semitic action. Grigoryev was a scoundrel, not fit to be included in the ranks of honest revolutionary workers. Grigoryev pulled out his pistol but was shot by Simon Karetnik with a Colt revolver. And then Makhno completed the execution. All of this before the eyes of the entire congress. Makhno spoke again. He took responsibility, which was his nature. He would accept the consequences.

"And that is the broom of Makhno," Marusya said. "To understand Makhno is to understand the revolution. No one is above the law. Death is not feared. The land is ours, not the

Bolsheviks'. We are called a motiveless terror. Nonsense. We are only called this because our motives do not agree with those who call us by this name."

It was late. Marusya walked to the fire and took up the pot and poured herself more tea. She returned to Sablin. "Are you listening?" she asked.

Sablin nodded.

She said that Makhno was a great general. Fearless. "Like our poet Shevchenko, he is loyal to Ukraine. Some say he is that way because he has nothing to lose. Not so. He is that way because he spent years in prison learning from the followers of Kropotkin, men like Arshinov, as I did, and now is the time for revenge. He loves his country and the peasant. That's all. It is love."

She was quiet. Sablin was quiet. Marusya had fallen asleep. He rose, and went to his bed in the stable, where he found Elizabeth. She was awake, waiting for him, shivering.

He sat at the edge of the bed. "What is it? Has something happened?"

She didn't talk. Her teeth chattered. He took her hand and lay down beside her, on the mat, fully clothed. He gathered her in his arms. So small. She cried then. And when she stopped, she said that she had seen him. The man. The one in the sailor's hat. At supper.

"What man? What did he do?"

"The men that attacked my village. He was with them. His smell. I know it."

"Are you sure? They all smell the same."

She sat up. "You don't know. You don't know smell like I do. It's him. The thumb on his right hand is gone. Go look."

She said that she was too ashamed to tell Sablin what the sailor did. Only to say that the man was evil. She was afraid.

He held her and said that the man would not hurt her again. Never. Eventually, she fell asleep. He heard the men calling out as they grew more drunk. He did not sleep. In the morning he rose early to find the men sleeping on the ground. Marusya slept by her horse, the reins tied to her foot. He walked amongst the men. Found the man in the sailor's hat and looked down upon him. He kicked at him. The man grunted and went back to snoring. He kicked him again. The man sat up and groped for his pistol. Sablin took it from him and pulled him to his feet. Dragged him past the stable and propped him by the fence. He went to wake Elizabeth. "Come tell me," he said. "Don't worry, he won't see you." He guided her to the edge of the door and showed her the man. Elizabeth stepped forward and approached the sleeping sailor and she leaned forward slightly and breathed and then pointed down at his right hand and turned to Sablin and said, "It is him."

"Go down to the root cellar, and stay there," Sablin said.

He gave her a blanket, helped her with her shoes, and pushed her in the direction of the cellar. When she had disappeared, he went to the stable where his stallion was hidden, and he saddled it. He tied the sailor's hands and feet and stood him and leaned him against the horse. The stallion shied and the sailor tumbled back to the ground. The sailor was unconscious. Sablin talked to the horse, said that all was good, that he would let no harm come to him. And then he stood the sailor against the horse one more time and heaved him up behind the saddle and balanced him there. He nearly slid over the other side. Sablin mounted and left the yard, the sailor behind him, one hand gripping the sailor's shirt. He rode a few miles and then cut down towards

the river. He dismounted and pulled the sailor from the horse.
He landed with a thump. Woke and called out. Sablin removed
the sailor's boots and took his pistol. He grabbed him by the
hair and pulled him down to the water. Walked in until he was
waist deep and then held the sailor's head under water. Much
thrashing, but Sablin was strong, and the sailor was very drunk.
The sailor was like a large fish that had suddenly been caught
and was now aware of the danger. He pummelled the water
and kicked and pummelled some more. Sablin sat on his torso
and twisted his neck. When the thrashing stopped, Sablin sat
for a few more minutes, as if finishing off the last of an early
morning bath. Finally, he rose and released the sailor and the
body floated slowly downstream.

When he rode into the yard, Marusya was building a fire.
She looked up. She was smoking. She came to him and touched
the stallion's withers and said, "Did you steal this one?"

"It is mine."

She said that his boots were wet. And his clothes.

"I went swimming with the sailor," he said. "But he was not
able to swim. Or he was too drunk." He said that the sailor
would not be riding with her anymore. He handed her the
sailor's boots, with the pistol tucked inside.

She studied him for a long time. She smoked. Then she said
that Sablin would replace the sailor.

He said that he would think about it.

"No thinking necessary," she said. "There is only one
answer. If you do not come, I will shoot the boy, Ens." And
she returned the pistol to him.

He went to Elizabeth and told her to stay hidden. He would
return within the week. That was certain.

"The sailor?" she asked.

"Gone," he said. He gave her the sailor's pistol. He showed her how to cock it, and the chamber where the bullets were inserted. He said that she should only use it if necessary. She didn't want it. She said that she couldn't.

"Think of the sailor," he said. "And then use it."

"I won't," she said, and pushed the pistol back into his hand.

At noon Marusya left with her men. They rode off with great shouts, and much noise, and the dust rose behind them and obscured the pale sky. Sablin, on his stallion, rode at the rear.

▶◀

There were two root cellars on the estate. The main cellar had half walls built from sod, and a staircase that descended to the doorway, which sat six feet beneath the surface of the earth. The door was small, upright, and led to an interior where more stairs dropped nine feet into the earth and the room inside was large and lined with shelves upon which sat clay jars of milk and cream and butter, and jars of canned fruit and vegetables. A smoked ham hock hung in the rear. Rings of sausages, made from pork and beef. And a table with bowls for developing film, used by Sablin. The bowls had been emptied. The cellar smelled of chemicals.

The second cellar was located beneath what used to be the manor kitchen. It was smaller, with a wooden trap door covered with soot, and a ladder that dropped through the opening to the small space below, where there was a half carcass of a cow and a slaughtered sow, yet to be smoked, and a few fresh vegetables, beans mostly, picked recently from the garden, and potatoes from last year's harvest.

Elizabeth was hiding in the smaller cellar. It was dark. There was a lamp, and a small tin of extra kerosene, but for the first night and into the next day Elizabeth did not light the lamp, as she feared that the light might creep out and be seen, even though the ground door was sealed. The last she saw of Sablin was his boots, and then the light disappeared, and she was in the dark, and faintly she heard horses, and voices calling out, and then a stampede nearby, more horses, and then silence. She did not open the door. It was cool and dry in the cellar, and after some time she felt the cold. She began to shiver. There was bedding straw on the dirt floor, and she gathered the straw and made a trough for herself and lay down and covered herself with the blanket Sablin had given her. She did not know what Sablin meant when he said that the sailor was gone. Gone where? South? North? Dead? And if dead, how so? She didn't believe Sablin could kill. He was too soft, too kind. And the woman on the white horse wouldn't have allowed it. The sailor would come back. She believed this. She slept and dreamed that the sailor was holding her throat and breathing into her mouth. He had six hands, all with no thumbs, and all six hands held her and touched her. She woke, shaking. She was very cold. She stood and found the ladder in the dark and pushed open the door slightly. It was night. There was nothing out there. An owl. Silence. And the owl again. She closed the door and slipped back down to cover herself. She shivered in the darkness, at some point realizing that she was completely alone, and even though Sablin had said he would return, she knew that he was gone. Perhaps completely gone.

She rose again and climbed the ladder and pushed open the door and this time she climbed out into the open air and stood near the opening. A warm breeze pushed against her.

It was quiet. The moon was half full. The trees in the orchard looked like men standing in rows. She told herself that these were simply trees. In the moonlight she walked to her hut and took a pillow and another blanket and a box of matches and she returned to the cellar and climbed inside and lit the lamp. Climbed the ladder and closed the door. She found a row of jars, full of honey. She opened one and the smell was lovely and made her teeth ache. She clawed at the honey and ate, sucked at her fingers, and then clawed for more. When she had enough, she turned off the lamp, lay down, and fell asleep with a finger in her mouth.

She heard a river flowing, trickling over rocks, picking up speed, tumbling into the thunder of rapids. She woke. Heard the rain hitting the door above her. She climbed the ladder and peeked into the open air. The rain was fierce, and it hit her face, but she didn't mind. She stood on the ladder and cleaned her face and hands and arms. Held one hand out and felt the sting of the drops. Men, horses, armies, marauders, they all hated the rain. This had been her experience, that when the rains came, the men stayed away. She went to the summer kitchen and built a fire. She thought that the smoke from the fire could not be seen with the rain, and the dark sky. She boiled water and bathed herself, standing half-naked in the shelter of the summer kitchen, while the rain pounded down. She was crying, scrubbing away at the sailor, and when she finally stopped scrubbing, she was no longer crying. Foolish to cry. To what end?

She was in the stable three days later, feeding the heifer and milking the cow, singing softly to herself to the rhythm of the rain, when she heard a shout and a shot. She startled and, in rising, kicked over the pail of milk. Through the doorway she saw a group of men, some mounted, some walking and guiding their horses, and one man in the summer kitchen, adding wood to the fire that she had built. She stepped back. Climbed the ladder to the loft and hid behind a stack of hay. She knew that she would not live but knew also that she didn't want to be found alive. The men were beneath her now, talking about the cow. She heard the heifer squeal, and then there was a shot, and another shot, and the squealing stopped.

Much later she smelled meat roasting. Loud voices. Much clamour. And then silence as they ate. And drinking, she thought, for the men were louder now. Darkness came, which was a relief, for now she was safer. She had not moved except to urinate in a corner and then crawl back behind the hay. At night she heard snoring below her. She waited until just before dawn, after the noises and talking had long stopped, and only then did she creep down the ladder to find herself confronting two men who lay in Sablin's bed, holding each other, fully clothed. Both were snoring. She slipped to the door of the stable and looked around. It was still drizzling. She saw one horse tethered by the summer kitchen, but no other men. She ran. Straight for the cellar. Pulled up the cellar door, stumbled down the ladder, reached up to pull the door shut, and then fell the rest of the way to the mud floor. She lay there, with a tremendous pain in her hip. She listened. Lay there. Did not move. Eventually, she crawled to her trough and covered her head with her blanket, and she waited. She did not sleep. Or if she did sleep, it was for a minute and then she sat upright and said, "Do not sleep." This happened several times. She lost track of herself, and she lost track of time and she lost track of where she was. She prayed to God. She prayed to Jesus. She prayed to

Sablin. She bit her fist to stop herself from crying out. She had no sense of time.

At some point she heard the fire, and she smelled smoke, and she heard a building collapse, though she did not know it was a building falling into itself until later, when she thought back and said to herself, That big noise was my hut collapsing. When she heard shouts, and the horses' hooves, she thought that now they were leaving, but she thought too that it was a trick, they would be waiting at the cellar door for her when she opened it, and so she waited until long after the sound of hooves had gone, and waited long after that, and then said, Wait, wait, wait, and so she waited and she used a bucket in the cellar as a toilet, and the smell was overwhelming, and she discovered that some straw laid inside the bucket removed the stench somewhat, but what was the smell of shit compared with the smell of those men? She ate honey. Slept some. Ate more honey. Tore with her teeth at a potato. Sablin had given her a bucket of water, and she drank from that, and each time she drank, she thanked Sablin, and God. She felt very close to God. Never had she believed in God as she did in that cellar. He was there beside her, and she felt at peace. Thank you, she said. She ate more honey. She pissed into the bucket. She used the straw. She woke to the sound of a horse neighing. A snort. Faint footsteps. She heard a voice. Her name. How could they know her name? She cowered. This was it. Again, her name, but this time in a familiar tone. Elizabeth. She stood at the bottom of the ladder. She stepped upwards. Pushed against the door. Saw Sablin's boot hanging from the side of a horse, but of course it wasn't Sablin, Sablin was dead, and then her name again, in Sablin's mouth, and she pushed the door upwards towards all that light, and she couldn't see.

The Druzhina, Marusya at the head, had left the Martens estate
and ridden to Alexandrovsk, and then over to Gulyai-Polye,
on the way entering the yard of what was a German Lutheran
estate that had obviously been pillaged previously, but even
so there was one sheep to slaughter, and a few chickens. The
manager of the estate was shot in the head, without discus-
sion. There was an older woman and two young women on
the estate. The older woman was taken out behind one of the
worker's houses by a short soldier in leather pants while the
younger women silently baked bread and made supper, their
eyes turned down. Marusya said nothing, appeared to not even
notice, and this being so, Sablin said nothing and did nothing.
Marusya wanted a photo of the very happy and well-fed team.
And then the man in leather pants wanted a singular photo,
just himself, holding his rifle. Sablin obliged him. At night
Sablin heard the women crying out, and in the morning he
found all three in the summer kitchen, their hair tied up in
kerchiefs, stoking the fire and cooking. Their faces were immut-
able, their hands moved in the same manner as they had the
night before. Which was something that Sablin came to recognize over the next weeks — that a woman who has been raped
the night before is still able to make breakfast in the morning.
On this morning the older woman noticed Sablin and, perhaps
seeing in his face something different, whispered to him that
her daughters had almost been taken the night before. What
should they do? Sablin said that they should continue as they
were. Bake bread, cook bacon, serve the men. "Obey them," he
said, "and you will live."

The woman looked at him and said, "Why are you with them?"

He turned away.

Over the next ten days he looked for an occasion to escape, but Marusya was vigilant. He showed no interest in killing, though he sometimes took photographs of the dead. Especially the dead animals, which moved him greatly. He felt much pity for the poor horses. The sun rose, the sun set. Rose again.

One night, when the men were very drunk, they laughed at Sablin and asked how many men he had killed. "Forty? Fifty? None?"

Sablin ignored them.

They called him a girl. A very tall and timid girl. A girl with muscles.

"Has anyone asked you to kill?" one of the men asked him.

He shook his head.

"We might, though," he said. "And then you will have to. How do you think you will stay alive? Either you kill or be killed."

Marusya was watching and listening and smiling and smoking. She was silent. One time, when passing him by, she had touched his head and said that he was beautiful. He had not responded. Though if she had asked something of him, he would have given what was required.

Life was mere chance. Martens taking him and Inna in and sending him to school, teaching him the ways of horses and livestock, giving him boots to wear. His love of Birr. Or was that love? Perhaps he might have loved Elsa just as ardently if she had allowed it. But he wasn't good enough. But for Birr he was, briefly, and for Andriy he was enough. Inna had once told him that he was too easygoing, that he would be taken advantage of, but this was a case of the sow calling the horse unclean. They were alike. Such was the nature of family, of brother and sister. There were moments, upon leaving a village or an estate, in the aftermath, that he saw the young women standing in the shadows or behind the trees in the orchards, and he thought of Inna, and he began to shake, and the shaking did not stop for a long time, not until the group was far down the road.

Around this time Sablin ran out of film for his Ango and so now his purpose had changed. In fact he had no purpose. That day Marusya and her men had come upon a small cavalry of Bolsheviks in retreat and had chased them for miles, catching up to them at the banks of a river. The Bolsheviks began to cross, their horses screaming, the air full of shouts. A *tachanka* carrying a machine gun was set up on the bank, almost leisurely, for the river was wide, and there was time. The chatter of the gun began, and the Bolsheviks fell. Those who were not shot were chased by Marusya's men and drowned in the river. Sablin, on his stallion, at the edge of the action. The men yelled at him to come have some fun. Far down the bank a lone Bolshevik had managed to clamber back onto dry ground. Marusya waved at Sablin and said, "Go." Sablin chased the Bolshevik down. It was a young boy, hardly sixteen. He carried nothing in his hands, no weapon. His boots were made of felt. He was very thin. He looked up at Sablin, mounted on the stallion, and he babbled. He made no sense. He removed his cap and pointed at the centre of his forehead and said, "Here, here." Sablin took his pistol, cocked it, and shot the boy in the head.

The loot was plenty. Boots, rifles, horses, ammunition. Marusya was most pleased with the ammunition. There was alcohol as well in one of the wagons and that night the men celebrated. A certain soldier, known for his dexterity, did somersaults over the fire. Gunshots were released into the air, until Marusya called for a halt. A dead horse was gutted and quartered and roasted over a large fire. Sablin was praised. He had finally killed. One man, Fedor, sat beside Sablin and leaned into him and whispered in his ear. This was not the first night Fedor had eyed Sablin. But it was the first time that he had come so close and been so intimate. "Drink," Fedor said, and handed him the bottle. Sablin shook his head. "You are very beautiful," Fedor whispered. In the darkness he took Sablin's hand and held it. He sighed. Drank. The men, one by one, fell asleep where they were sitting, their heads lolling. Some slid sideways and lay on the ground by the fire. Fedor said that he would bite Sablin's ear. He stabbed with his mouth at Sablin, missed, and fell with his face in Sablin's lap. He groaned. Chuckled. Tried to lift himself. Sablin took Fedor's head and shifted it onto the ground and straightened Fedor's legs. He was immediately snoring. Across the fire Marusya watched. She smoked. She said nothing. Maybe she smiled, it was hard to tell. Sablin matched her gaze. Finally, she stood and walked to her horse, tied the reins to her ankle, and laid herself out on the ground. She sang to herself then, her voice ragged and not terribly clear. The tune and words were familiar to Sablin. Apples rolling on the ground. Tolya used to sing the same song. For an hour she sang, her voice getting weaker. And then she stopped. Still Sablin sat, Fedor sleeping beside him, the other men stirring and moving but not waking. How easy it would be to slaughter them all, thought Sablin.

Just before dawn he rose and stood silently over the dead fire. He waited for someone to notice him. Nothing. He moved then, very slowly, going out to where the horses were tethered

in the dark. He found his horse. He didn't saddle him. He took
him by the mane and guided him past the other horses and out
into the darkness. He expected to hear shouts, men calling,
perhaps shots fired. Nothing. There was no moon, the darkness
was complete. A mile from the encampment he mounted his
horse and leaned forward and whispered in his ear to go slow.
Slow. The horse obeyed. He had no reins, no saddle. Only the
halter, which he held as he talked to the horse. Slowly at first,
and then at a canter, and finally, as the sun rose, at a gallop, he
rode north, towards Chortitza, a deserter.

He arrived late morning at the estate, the horse frothing
and exhausted. The stable was gone, torn down. The corrals
and fences destroyed. Elizabeth's hut had been burned. The
haystacks burned. Only the summer kitchen remained. He
rode up to the entrance of the root cellar and called Elizabeth's
name. Called again. He waited for a long time, looking around
at the destruction. Then, as he was about to dismount, the door
of the root cellar pushed upwards and a face appeared, small
and pale. She said nothing at first. Was blinded by the morning
sun. Then she said, "I stink."

He fed and watered the horse, and then built a fire in
the summer kitchen, drew water from the well, and boiled
the water. There was an old tub in the orchard, and he took
that and mixed hot water with the cold and tested it with his
wrist. He told her to clean herself. He walked down into the
orchard and inspected the trees, which were full of small fruit.
He stood and looked out at the fields where the winter wheat
Tolya had planted in the fall had headed and was filling out.
Come August it would require harvesting, but that meant
workers and horses, and machines, and workers were few, or
afraid, and Martens's threshing machine had been stripped

by local villagers. The vegetable garden was flourishing. The beans were ready to pick. He found the cow bellowing at the edge of the orchard, swollen with milk. He roped it and pulled it home and milked it. Cleaned out the root cellar and got rid of the night soil. Went to find Elizabeth, who had put on one of Irmgard's dresses. It was too large, but she had cinched the waist with a rope. Her eyes were wet. Her hair as well. She said that she'd thought he was dead. And that she would die. The men had come at night and taken and taken. But they had not discovered the roof to the cellar. She had prayed. And God had answered her prayers.

7.

BLACK NIGHT

Wiebe, a neighbour to Lehn and Inna, was keeping a diary. It was written in German, and the first entry was from September 1914 and the diary carried through until the present, summer of 1919. The entries were factual, a record of local events and sometimes of world events. 15-12-14: "Already we have been forbidden to preach in German in our churches." 19-6-14: "All pigeons were registered by the police. They are looking for carrier pigeons." And so on. Wiebe mentioned the diary one evening when he and Lehn were playing checkers and talking about the latest movement of troops through the village. He said, "I'm an accountant. I like to keep track of things. For example, the price of wheat today has risen two thousand percent from when I first began the diary. And the dead. I note the dead. Which Maria dislikes. She thinks we should remain positive. I believe we have brought the suffering upon ourselves. We have taken up arms and provoked the enemy." He shook his head.

Wiebe had been married three times. The first time for nine months. The second for three years. The first two wives had died tragically, of typhus and during childbirth. His third marriage, to Maria Lietz, a sister to the first two, had taken place ten years ago. They had six children, two from his second marriage, and so the eldest two children now had their aunt as their stepmother. Wiebe was originally a teacher who was now the bookkeeper at the Chortitza Bank. He often talked about his older children, and what they were studying. Lehn found him affable. He was self-critical, a pacifist, a Christian who had no wish to convert Lehn, and he appreciated poetry. He hadn't before meeting Lehn, but now in the evenings Lehn would foist some Pushkin on him, and Wiebe was surprisingly open. He liked to say that a farmer who read poetry was like the goose who sat down to eat with the fox. "Highly impractical." But there was something true in Pushkin. He liked "The Bronze Horseman" and literally likened it to the siege and assault of the present day — God's great wrath, the wrecks of huts, the logs, roofs' pieces, waiting for death, and how to live.

Lehn smiled and allowed him his joy.

Lehn was now spending more time in Rosental. Ekaterinoslav was under constant siege, and sales of books were dwindling. No one had money, and if they did, it was for food and firewood. Karine was gone. Living with her mother. Inna had asked about her once since his return, and Lehn had said that she was departed.

"Dead?" Inna asked.

"No, just gone."

"Oh."

Lehn smiled. "You want her dead."

"Of course not. I was just curious."

"And still jealous."

"Should I be?"

"You are my wife. I am your husband. That is enough."

Lehn had managed to carry some of his favourite books back to Rosental by droshky, and on the evenings he sat with Wiebe, and as they talked or played checkers, he would suggest something other than Pushkin poetry, a novel perhaps, but Wiebe said that he wasn't romantic enough for novels. "I'll leave that to your type."

Inna, on the evenings when Lehn subjected Wiebe to a bit of reading, laughed and said that this was how Lehn wooed his women.

Wiebe said that poetry was foreign to him.

Lehn asked if he liked the Psalms.

"Of course."

"That is poetry."

"It is the Bible."

"Poets wrote the Bible."

"Prophets."

"Poets are prophets."

Wiebe did not smile often, but at this he smiled. He said that it was strange to be talking like this when outside, throughout the country, people were being killed. For no reason.

Lehn said that the only thing that kept him alive during this madness were his books. "There is nothing else in life."

"Only a romantic would say that," Wiebe said. "What about bread? Horses? Cattle? Food? A house? You don't need those things?"

Inna, who liked to be part of the conversation, said that for Lehn the soul was more important than the body.

"We agree, then," Wiebe said. "But to sustain the soul, you must sustain the body."

Lehn nodded. "But most of us only want to sustain the body. We do not care about the soul."

Wiebe lit a cigarette. He smoked. And was quiet. And then he said, "Soda for soap now costs forty rubles, and thread fifty rubles. This afternoon, four young soldiers came in and insisted they wanted shoes. I gave them foot rags made from a sack. They weren't happy. And then were happy enough. How much do we need to make us happy? I think Mennonites have brought the wrath of God upon their own heads. Now we use guns to protect our bodies, and we forget our souls. You are right, Lehn. You are right about the soul. Do you know something we don't?"

Inna smiled. "You will swell his head if you tell him he is right."

They drank coffee ground from barley.

Inna said that her brother, Sablin, was coming for a visit. He and a girl named Elizabeth were the only ones now living on the Martens estate. Though supposedly there was nothing left to run. "Perhaps he will marry Elizabeth. He says they are like brother and sister. She is young."

The men heard her but did not respond. Lehn thought that Inna could use more soap in the house. But then she would just use it to wash her pig. Yesterday a cavalcade of Reds had come through the village, pushing the black army south. Two Reds had billeted at their house. They were polite. They ate, they slept, they did not complain, they did not bother Inna. Though they used all the soap to wash themselves, naked in the barn, very loud, very lewd. Lehn had a way with them, especially when he said that he had fought on the front near Czernowitz and had escorted a commissar to Petersburg. They were young, had seen war for only two months, and believed that the best part, the most glamorous battles, had already passed. They had missed out. They ate the potatoes that Inna had boiled, and they asked Lehn questions about the front. He looked them in the eyes and said that there was nothing glorious about war.

On a Tuesday, Lehn went up to Ekaterinoslav by droshky to look in on his bookshop with plans to carry a substantial number of books back to Rosental. He slept in the small room above the shop. The windows had all been destroyed by the bombing. The roof to the apartment was caved in, and rain had leaked through to the shop below. Many of the books were destroyed. He found what was salvageable, planning to return to Rosental the following day. On that morning two men entered the shop. They wore long leather jackets, little blue ribbons like a badge, red pants, carried Mausers, and wore polished black boots and soft officer caps. Chekists. They had entered his shop before and asked him questions, each question implying that he might lack loyalty to the Bolsheviks, but he answered and said that he had fought with the Red Army, he was fiercely patriotic to Russia, and to Lenin, and nothing would convince him otherwise. This time the questions were more pointed.

The taller one did the talking.

"Your class?"

"I am a renter. I own nothing."

"But you sell books."

"They are everyone's books. Please, help yourself."

"Your origin?"

"My family is from Odessa."

"Jewish?"

"I have no faith."

"And if I asked the woman you live with?"

"There is no woman here."

"Did you fight?"

"Yes."

"A deserter?"

"I have a letter from Commissar Shklovsky showing my discharge." He said, "Besides this, I am old. And blind in one eye."

"Which eye?"

"The right." He forced himself to hold that eye open and he projected it upwards to the ceiling and held it there.

The tall one waved this away. "Education?" he asked.

"Half a year of university, and then I left out of disillusionment, and I raised birds."

"Birds. What kind of birds?"

"Goldfinches."

"A business, then."

"A hobby. I made nothing on the birds. They became my breakfast."

These men had no sense of humour, Lehn thought. He must be more serious.

"And your profession now?" the tall man asked.

"The bookshop is finished. I am returning to my village to plant a crop."

"Now, at this time of year?"

"Winter wheat," Lehn said. He knew this much.

"Do you own a house, a barn, livestock?"

"I rent a small house in Rosental. I know nothing about livestock."

"And the land for the winter wheat?"

"Rented as well."

"And this shop?"

"Not mine."

"Who owns it?"

"A man named Martens. He is now in Kiev."

"The books?"

"They are yours, they are mine, they are for whoever wants them."

"You have how many books?"

"I haven't counted."

The tall one looked around and said, "We are of the opinion that a man does not need more than five books. You have hundreds." And then he asked if Lehn knew Blok.

"The poet?" Lehn asked.

"Is there another?"

"Do you recommend him?" Lehn asked.

The tall one became agitated. He said that Lehn was the bookseller, the recommender of poets and scribblers. It appeared that Lehn might be a little too sophisticated. "You speak carefully, with the lilt of an intellectual."

Lehn said that he wasn't an intellectual. He admired men like Lenin, whose voice came from the soil, like the peasant.

"So Lenin is now a peasant."

"Does Lenin not love the peasant? Speak for the peasant?"

The tall one looked at the shorter man, who was walking around the shop, leaning forward to study various spines. He was smoking and peering. The tall one said that of course Lenin spoke for all. "Be very careful, Mr. Lehn," he said.

Lehn looked out at the street, and then said that he would take that advice. It was good advice. He only wanted to be conscious of the new, and the good, and the future.

The tall one nodded. He said that he needed papers for rolling cigarettes. Would Lehn mind? He picked up the copy of *Dyadya Vanya*.

"Of course, no problem. But those pages are too thick. Try this one," Lehn said, and he handed him a thin book with thin pages, written by a poet who had died long ago.

The tall one touched the pages of the dead poet and said that these would do.

When they had left, Lehn sat down on a pile of books. He breathed slowly, swallowing so as not to vomit. Armoured cars passed by in the street. Men marching. The machines of war had become so common that it no longer registered in his mind. He saw the guns, the cannons, the marching columns of men, as a silhouette, objects enveloped in a sack. It was as if everyone around him was living unconsciously, like those two men who had come in and recited their questions, not with any curiosity, but in order to catch him out, to trap him, and in their questions they had seemed unconscious, and if one went on unconsciously, then it was as if you had never been. And so, life became nothing. One's work, clothes, furniture, books, one's wife — all passed like a wisp of smoke.

He had the Blok poem, *The Twelve*. It was tucked away. He hadn't known what the right answer was. Which was the point. Uncertainty. Fear. Black night. White snow. The wind, the wind! Impossible to stay on your feet.

Later that evening, back in Rosental, he undressed Inna and touched her and said, "Your nose, your mouth, your hair falling past your ears here, and down to your shoulders here, and your clavicle here, and your ribs showing here, your chest too thin here, your hips here, your thighs here, your knees and calves here, your feet here." He placed two fingers on the inside of her right wrist and said, "Ba bump. Ba bump. Ba bump."

She laughed and said, "You love me."

◄►

Sablin and Elizabeth visited Lehn and Inna on a Sunday in fall, arriving on a battered droshky that Sablin had repaired and made travel worthy. Sablin had hired a local boy of fifteen whom he trusted to milk the cow and feed the chickens. They had left early morning. The White Army was on the east bank of the Dnieper. Makhno and his men and whoever else ran with them were on the west bank. The two armies eyed each other and sometimes fired cannons to remind themselves and others that they existed. It was dangerous to cross the river near Chortitza and so Sablin went further south, and he and Elizabeth crossed by ferry. Inna called them mad and lucky, and she held Elizabeth tightly and said, "So you are taking care of my Sablin." Elizabeth said that it had nothing to do with luck and it was God's job to take care of Sablin, though she didn't mind lending a hand. Sablin said nothing, just watched the interaction and then went off with Lehn to replace a few windowpanes in the kitchen with bits of salvaged glass. At lunch Wiebe dropped by and stood in the doorway and said that thirty orphans were being sent down to Tokmak, where families would take them in. He said that the hardest part was separating children who came from the same family. Also, there were evangelistic services planned for that week. Tent missionaries from Odessa were passing through. They had been given free passage by Makhno. "One corner of his soul has some light creeping through," he said. He left.

Sablin had tiny drawers in his head and some of those drawers he kept shut — the sailor, the women crying out at night, baby Katka, Marusya, the sixteen-year-old boy, Makhno. And now, hearing Makhno's name, a drawer opened slightly, and he slammed it shut. And opened the drawers that held Inna, and the vegetable garden, and Elizabeth, who sat across from him, her hands folded on the table. Elizabeth, who was only sweetness and light. No evil there. The small finger on her left hand had some dirt under the nail and he reached out and covered her small hand with his large one. She looked at him and smiled.

Inna was watching. She said that they would have to marry soon, the two of them. "You can't pretend to be brother and sister forever."

Lehn laughed. "This from a woman who shared a house with me for a year unmarried."

"We told people we were married," Inna said. "Sablin and Elizabeth have said no such thing."

Lehn said that love and marriage cured the spleen, and he gave a little speech about sentiment, which was a subtler form of love.

"But we aren't married," Elizabeth said. "And we do live as brother and sister. Why would we lie?" She pulled her hand out from under Sablin's and said to him, "Come with me. To the services this week. We can stay with Inna and Lehn. Yes?"

"Of course," Inna said.

On that first night of services, when the missionaries called out for those who were sinners to lay their burden down and give their souls to Jesus, Sablin stood with many others. Elizabeth stood beside him and took his hand. The preacher called out that the lowliest had now become mighty, and the mightiest had fallen. "In the world to come, so the last shall be first, and the first last: for many be called, but few chosen."

The following morning Elizabeth whispered in Inna's ear that Sablin had stood the night before. He now wanted to be baptized. Her face glowed. She clutched Inna's arm. They returned to the estate that afternoon, with promises of another visit. Elizabeth held Sablin's hand in the wagon on the way home. He told her that he was very fond of her, and that he would always stay by her side, as long as she wished him to, but only as a brother. "You don't know what is in my heart," he said. She said that she could see his heart, and it was a good heart, and she would wait for him. On a Sunday the preacher from Village #3 rode out to baptize them. Elizabeth's hair was growing out again, and her face was smaller and frailer. Her hair was blond and had a slight wave to it, and when it was clean, it shone in a certain light. Sablin was aware of her. But he was also aware of himself.

◄►

When Inna told Lehn that Sablin was now a Christian and that the path was now clear for a wedding, Lehn was bemused. The ways of the church, the neighbours, the rules they followed or didn't follow, the subjection of mind to soul, the primacy of what these people called faith, the language about Jesus, the conflation of sexuality and salvation, of peace and violence, he had witnessed all of this before. It was curious, and sometimes convincing, and other times he saw the hypocrisy, and the severity, and he saw himself as a stranger to this world. Inna not so much. She was easier. More flexible. She got along with Goerzen. Loved to gossip. Laughed easily. Never gave in to despair. Rarely looked at herself in the mirror. And this would keep her alive.

Wiebe came by every evening now, and he and Lehn talked late into the night. Wiebe liked to recite facts, to offer up the latest news as if it had some bearing on how to live. He preferred the Cossacks to the Makhnovists though both were unpredictable and stunk. He disliked the Reds most of all, and was hoping that the White Army would return, or perhaps the Germans. He planned to emigrate. He was looking into getting papers for his family. Four Reds were shot in Hochfeld, no one knew by whom. Fifty-five thousand rubles had been requisitioned by the local soviet. Some soldiers had come to eat at their house. Maria had fed at least twenty-five men. They had been quite reasonable except for one soldier who insisted on having Wiebe's shoes. "I gave him an extra pair and Maria sent them off with buns. Are we mad to think that generosity and non-violence will save us? Only God can save us."

"What I have noticed," Lehn said, "is that non-violence is very handy. Because then one doesn't have to carry a gun and march to the front, and one can work in forestry, or as a medic, all very selfless endeavours.

"And the memoir?" Lehn asked.

Wiebe said that it was a record keeping, not a memoir. "Do not flatter me."

Lehn talked about the commissar he had escorted to Petersburg. That he, like Wiebe, had been writing a memoir. "Though you see the world differently. The commissar's convictions were secular, and he was a soldier. Though he might have fed the soldiers as you do and given them shoes. I can't know. You, Wiebe, believe in God. You are both a fatalist and a pacifist. Or perhaps a pacifist is always a fatalist."

Wiebe said that it had nothing to do with fatalism. It was a belief. A faith. It wasn't about selflessness. "Violence has never cured the world. Look around you. Man is evil. Greedy. Full of lust and vengeance. I cannot stand with vengeance. Even if it costs me my life. Our men, who arm themselves? Take Heinrichs in Eichenfeld. I don't recognize that kind of man, the one who carries a gun and leads a civilian army and wears a uniform so proudly. Just last week his men shot four Makhnovists. Without provocation. An eye for an eye will never work. Mark my words. They are disobeying the teachings of Christ. Which are to turn the other cheek."

◄►

The men came more frequently now, at all hours, but usually at dusk, when they were hungry or angry or greedy or tired. Plundering at night was always simpler, as if the shell of darkness might hide their works. They came on foot, on the backs of horses both saddled and bare, on wagons pulled by black beasts, on donkeys, in a car once, on a bicycle stolen from a neighbour, on bare feet, black boots, hobbling, running, laughing, drinking, hands raw, black eyes, wearing black, sometimes red, but mostly black, carrying guns, swords, kitchen knives, carrying the dust of the road, demanding everything, but often food. "Make us bread." They ate at the tables in the dining room, sometimes in the summer kitchen, seated on chairs or on pillows, calling for more, as if they had just arrived home after a long voyage and were demanding what was deserved. And in the morning they left, having traded for fresh horses, or not traded at all but simply taken, gathering up buns and butter, a last swipe at a passing bottom, a guttered stab, and leaving behind them silence, save for the quiet weeping of the young girl in the attic. Only to return two days later.

A woman of twenty-five, who has three or four children, whose husband has just come in from working the fields, and for whom she has made soup and fresh bread and a dessert of plum platz, that woman, who grew up with a father similar to her husband, and a church that taught self-sufficiency, and hard work, and peace, and non-violence, that woman has no idea who or what these soldiers represent or what they want, or why they come one day and violate everything that is sacred, and then leave with much noise, a vacuum of silence in their passing, and only to return the following day, or the next week, or if they don't come back, some other group appears, but smelling the same, talking the same, taking the same. This woman has no overt politics, though it might aid her if she did, and if her husband is a landowner, if he has earth that he calls his own, he might be shot, or he might live, but he will probably be killed, because he is a kulak who took what was not rightfully his, or he will be killed because he is in the wrong place. This woman has no habit or skill that would allow her to understand the workings of the world. She cries out, "Who are you? What do you want?" and she is scorned. And when she is taken upstairs into the attic, she goes meekly, without looking back, and when she returns, she doesn't look her husband in the eye. She looks at his boots, and then her shoes, which she never removed in the attic, such was the ignominy. This woman, as a witness, could not identify her attacker, certainly not by name, or rank, or uniform, or loyalty, or government, or team, or army, or country. He spoke Ukrainian, he spoke Russian, he spoke German, he spoke Armenian, Turkish, he didn't speak. But she knew his smell, and the noises he made, and the shape of his teeth and ears.

News came through Wiebe that Makhnovists had surrounded the village of Eichenfeld, blocked off both ends of the village, slaughtered seventy-five men and boys, killed five tent missionaries, raped the women and girls, burned down houses, and run off with every object possible. Heinrichs had been the first to be shot. Wiebe thought that the Bolsheviks were pushing the Makhnovists south, and this was their death rattle. "If only." He said that a wild dog that senses the end will kill everything around it.

Inna suggested to Lehn that they should go stay with Sablin and Elizabeth, that it might be safer on the estate than here in the village. Normally so hopeful and positive, she was now frightened. Lehn said that if she wanted to go, they could try, but to cross the river was to invite being shot, and besides, they couldn't take Salo with them. They would have to slaughter her before leaving.

Inna turned away and immediately went out to talk to her sow.

The rest of that day and into the evening it was quiet, no cavalcades or riders demanding sustenance, buns, or beds in which to sleep. Lehn read. It was cold outside, with a light rain, and there was a fire in the stove. The blankets were in the warming oven. Inna was mending clothes, sometimes saying that she was sad for Salo, and then asking Lehn to read to her, which he did. When she left the room to get something, he continued reading to himself, only to pick up with her when she returned. He sometimes put the book in his lap — it was the short works of Tolstoy — and when he did so, he was aware of the rain falling towards the south windows, and the smell of the woodsmoke, and he said to Inna that he might be getting nostalgic, she should be aware. She asked what he meant by nostalgic, and he said that he wasn't sure, except that something inside him, in his heart or mind, kept recalling his childhood, which hadn't been terribly bad, but not good either. "My father when he was happiest read at his desk, the book pressed flat, his head bent forward. He had poor eyesight but refused to wear glasses. My mother, when she caught him reading, told him he was lazy, and he immediately put the book down and stood at attention, waiting for orders, but no orders came, and so he stood there, his hands clasped, sneaking glances at his book."

"Do I give you orders?" Inna asked.

"Never."

Inna said that Goerzen had offered to help with the slaughter the next day. She was experienced. She rose and gathered the warm blankets. "Come to bed, Lehn," she said. He closed the lamp and joined her.

At two a.m. there were gunshots over in the direction of Wall's yard. Screams. A dog barking. Inna ran out to the barn in her nightshift and hid. Lehn followed but stopped first to gather his glasses and pants. He put them on and stumbled out the door and ran into a young man, very young, too young, who wore felt boots and rags as clothes, and who carried a Nagant. He asked if Lehn had rubles or a wife or a daughter or bread. Boots. He held the Nagant to Lehn's head. Lehn said that he lived alone. He had no rubles, but he had bread. The young boy calmed down. He muttered and pushed Lehn back through the doorway. Was Lehn the owner? No. Did Lehn own anything? A horse? A pig? No animals. Only some blankets, utensils for the kitchen. A few books. Nothing. Just books. The young man became agitated. He began to yell that books would not help him. And where was his wife? And look, look, there was a dress. Did Lehn wear a dress? "I won't eat books," the young man said. He asked for Lehn's glasses. Lehn handed them to the boy, and he put them on. He squinted, seeking out the objects around him. And then he raised the gun and pulled the trigger and shot Lehn in the head.

Inna hid in the barn, lying behind the manger that held the grain for the cow. Someone entered. A young boy in felt boots. Inna held a hand over her mouth as the soldier struggled to have sex with Salo, both squealing, a terrible inferno, and finally the boy gave up and slit Salo's throat. Panting. A grunt. The voice of a girl singing plaintively in the neighbouring yard.

8.

THE FAT EARTH

Though they were not married, and slept in separate huts, Sablin and Elizabeth talked as intimately as husband and wife and conferred on every decision they made. In March they asked Inna to move out to the estate to live with them. On the same day that they picked up Inna, they also collected the two Goerzen daughters, Leah and Rachel, whose parents had been killed the same night as Lehn. Leah had stopped speaking, but Rachel made up for it by talking and singing non-stop. Sablin, Elizabeth, and Inna rode the front bench of the wagon, and Rachel and Leah sat on the bed of the carriage with the chickens, a few chairs, blankets, Goerzen's wardrobe of dresses, kitchen utensils, a goose and gander, window frames and the glass, still intact, some of Lehn's books, and Inna and Lehn's bed. The cow followed, pulled along by a rope.

Sablin had built two huts on the estate, using the salvaged wood from the main house. The windows taken from Lehn's house would provide light and protection from the elements. One hut was for Inna and Rachel, and the other for Elizabeth and Leah, who clung to Elizabeth and wouldn't let her out of her sight. Each hut had a small stove for warmth. An outhouse stood back from the huts. The well was still producing fresh water. The two root cellars had been organized and cleaned. Earlier in the month Sablin had gathered deadfall in the stand of trees nearby and had chopped enough wood to carry them through the year. He had rebuilt the stable, and he slept near the remaining livestock — two cows, a single heifer, a goat, chickens, and a sow that he had received from a Ukrainian villager who was planting wheat on a strip of Martens's land. Other villagers, when they heard of this arrangement, came to Sablin and said they would plant as well. Sablin did not argue. He suggested that they divide the land between those who wanted it, and that they help each other with the seeding, and come harvest they would do the same, work together. Because the Bolsheviks were requisitioning surplus grain, they would plant only enough for their families. Some of the villagers thought that Sablin was too officious, and that he shouldn't be giving commands. Others saw him as necessary and welcomed Sablin's advice, whose voice was one of resignation and reason: we own nothing, we share everything, what's mine is yours, we do not hoard, we barter, we work for what we eat, if one is hungry then the other must feed him. Since his conversion he had become fond of quoting Scripture. "Lay not up for yourselves treasures upon earth, where moth and rust doth corrupt, and where thieves break through and steal." Sometimes, when Inna listened to him, or watched him work, she was reminded of Martens, in both the moral seriousness and the tenacity in his work. Like Martens he was tireless.

Martens would not return. Gossip had it that the remaining family had fled to Finland, or that they had been arrested and sent north. No one had heard from them. Sablin had no interest in gossip or hearsay. He was too busy repairing the steam thresher, and forging new wheels for the wagon, and planning, along with Elizabeth, a silkworm production. Come spring they would make use of the mulberry trees in the forest. Leah, the elder Goerzen daughter, attached herself to Sablin and followed him around the estate, helping him with his work. She was good with the axe and liked to split logs. He talked to her, explaining what he was fixing, even though she did not talk back. Her hands got involved. She had fierce love for the brood goose, and in the evenings, at supper, she would announce the laying of another egg by making a goose sound and flapping her arms. After the number seven the announcements halted, and she went silent again. She kept vigil, though. Sablin saw her crouched near the goose, who showed an abnormal acquiescence towards the presence of the young girl squatting nearby. They appeared at some points to be talking to each other. And when the eggs hatched in late April, the seven goslings followed Leah around the land, the mother at the rear.

Inna insisted on teaching the girls in the mornings. She had them sit in chairs, at a table in one of the huts, and she read to them from Lehn's books, and then had them write for themselves in various forms — diary, letter, essay — and one time Leah wrote a play about a girl who woos a mute boy, and so the play was essentially a monologue for the girl, played by Rachel. They presented the play one evening. It was well-received. Inna also taught them math and read them Greek myths from one of Lehn's books. The girls did not know these myths and fell for them hard. When the weather warmed, they went swimming in the creek. Inna called this physical education. After the swim she braided the girls' hair. And then her own.

◂▸

Wiebe visited and brought news of the village and the surrounding area. Half of the farms had been abandoned. The Reds were pushing the Whites south. Still, soldiers arrived demanding food and horses and grain for the horses. The uncertainty of the previous year's raids had abated. The arbitrary and senseless killing had mostly stopped, though there were still farmers being questioned and sometimes killed. Horses were still being requisitioned and so it would be difficult to harvest. There would be a famine. Wiebe had brought with him the hide of his dappled nag, and he gave it to Sablin to make shoes for the girls. Leah, who had begun to speak a few words again, indicated on a piece of paper the cut of shoe she wanted. And of course Rachel wanted the same style. If possible, perhaps they might have two pairs each, one for weddings, the other for every day. The girls had been boldly predicting that Elizabeth and Sablin would be married by summer. This clearly pleased Elizabeth, but she knew Sablin was hesitant. She told Inna that he needed a good kick in the pants. And that kick turned out to be the wedding of Nastja Volkova, a former servant on the Martens estate. All were invited. The girls wore their new shoes, and dresses sewn by Elizabeth, made from the cloth of Goerzen's dresses. The wedding took place in the Orthodox church, with festivities continuing at the bridegroom's farm just outside Alexandrovsk. The girls observed the dancing and ran in circles, showing off their shoes. Sablin sat on a wooden bench, Elizabeth at his side. She took his hand and said that a wedding was a good thing. "What are you afraid of, Sablin?"

He smiled and said, "Myself."

"Trust me," she said.

The following day an enormous column of men and wagons and large guns and horses passed by on the road bordering the estate, heading south. No one bothered to enter the yard of the estate, which was not surprising, as it looked abandoned and the burned timbers from the manor house still rose like blackened crosses into the sky. The earth moved for a long time after the troops had passed by. But this was not everyone, for a group of thirty stragglers entered the estate and watered their horses and asked for grain. Sablin obliged. They asked for food. The women baked buns and made soup. The men ate. They were polite. They said that they were just Russian soldiers, not Bolsheviks. Sablin's stallion was tied to the fence near the orchard and the officer in charge noted the stallion's lines and his strength and said that he would take him. Sablin went to his horse and whispered in his ear and then delivered the stallion to the officer. In exchange the officer gave Sablin his gelding, worn out and thin.

At supper, taken at the table near the summer kitchen, Elizabeth touched Sablin's hand and said that she was sorry about his horse.

Sablin said that it was just a horse. "We will fatten up the nag and she will work for us. Why do I need a fast and beautiful stallion anymore? I am a farmer."

Rachel said that Elizabeth was beautiful. Didn't Sablin think so? She too was a farmer.

Inna told Rachel to eat. "Mind yourself," she said. Rachel grinned at Elizabeth, and Elizabeth smiled back.

Sablin was practical. He took what was in front of him and accepted it. He was not nostalgic, he was not sentimental, and this gave him a great capacity for love.

That night Sablin knocked on the door to Elizabeth's hut, and when she answered, he said, "Walk with me."

They were married on August 26 at the edge of the orchard on the estate. Wiebe and his wife and children were present. Nastja and her husband. Some of the villagers who farmed with Sablin as well. Three of Elizabeth's sisters, including Elsa and her husband and child. A simple wedding, no alcohol, no dancing. The Goerzen girls flanked Sablin and Elizabeth, in their new shoes, and their dresses. Pastor Krahn questioned the bridal couple, blessed them, and then led everyone in song. The photographer from Rosental was present and Sablin paid him in kind, with a gift of an Ango camera. Rachel sang a solo.

Inna helped serve food with the other women. Elizabeth called out to her to come and sit, come eat with us, but Inna laughed lightly and said that she wanted to help. She did not say that her mind was elsewhere. Wiebe had found her just before the wedding ceremony and handed her a letter that had arrived from Lehn, written long ago when he had been at the front. It had come to the post office in Rosental recently, and it was Wiebe — having received it from Kliewer, the midwife's husband, and who took care of the post office — who was delivering it to her. Inna took the letter from Wiebe and slipped away and held it, unopened. She pushed the letter up inside the waist of her dress. During the service, and while she served food with the women, she felt the letter against her skin. She thought that she would never open it. That she would hold it in suspension. What was the point? But she was also curious, and practical, and so she waited until the next day, when she was alone, to read the letter. Many of the sentences had been blacked out. She tried to decipher them, even holding a candle up behind the paper to see the outline of the letters, but she saw nothing. The words that remained were a jumble, fragmented, much about food, and his clothing, and the books he had found and was reading, and then a line about an old Galician woman, and a mention of a book given him by a German soldier, poetry by Rilke, and much of the poem was blacked out, though the initial lines remained, "You didn't know what was in the heap." Finally, just before Lehn's salutation, "I kiss your little hand," there was a concluding and complete block of sentences. This was unedited. She read that final paragraph, and then, because she was still hungry, she read it again and again. She traced the letters with her finger, and she smelled the pages, but that was not enough, and so she ended up reading the words aloud to herself. And again.

> I have new boots. Not in great shape, but they are now
> mine, taken from the feet of a soldier who died just
> after arriving at the hospital. When I saw them, I took
> them off and exchanged them for the worn ones with
> holes that I was wearing, very strange to be slipping
> boots onto the feet of a man who no longer needed
> them. If I were religious I would say a miracle, but
> I believe only in nature and the material world, and
> boots being the essence of the material world, I see
> it as fate, and a sign of good luck, for now I picture
> myself walking home to you, to your blue eyes that
> I see in the sky as I walk, the clicking of my heels
> against stones and wood, sweet the fat earth, walking
> east and then south, pushing on, towards the living,
> you, you, you, and away from the dead.

JULIUS LEHN	d. 1919 Ukraine
INNA LEHN	d. 1921 Ukraine
SABLIN MARTENS	d. 1957 Canada
ELIZABETH MARTENS	d. 1978 Canada
KATKA MARTENS (daughter of Sablin and Elizabeth)	d. 1923 Ukraine
JULIUS MARTENS (son of Sablin and Elizabeth)	d. 2018 Canada
RACHEL GOERZEN	d. 1975 Canada
LEAH GOERZEN	d. 2000 Canada

Author's Note

Two books were essential to the writing of this novel: *A Sentimental Journey: Memoirs 1917–1922* by Viktor Shklovsky and *Troubles and Triumphs, 1914–1922* by Peter J. Dyck. The two books exist at opposite ends of the literary spectrum — Shklovsky was a Russian formalist who published novels, memoir, and literary criticism; Dyck was a Mennonite farmer from Ladekopp, Molotschna Colony, Ukraine, who kept a diary that was subsequently translated and published by his family in Canada. Shklovsky is sophisticated; he disguises his art with an effortless detachment. He is humorous, light of touch, and aware of the absurdity of war. Dyck's diary is objective and straightforward, and not at all self-conscious. His voice is very clear, and he sees the world around him through the objects that are given and taken. He talks a lot about boots and shoes. About food. About the bare necessities of existence. He lists the dead. There is no self-absorption, though he has a dry resignation. His last entry, 29-6-1924, is written as the family is about to leave Russia for Canada:

"Arrived at the border station of Sebesh. Stopped here for an entire day. All our property was thoroughly inspected. That night, at the border, all 'crown property,' such as ladders for climbing up into the car, wash basins, axes, saws and pails were taken from us. So again, and for the last time in Russia, we were robbed, just as we had been on the last night in Ladekopp. It all seemed quite natural."

Endnotes

The deserter scene, page 118; the quote including "Stendhal's Waterloo and Tolstoy's battle scenes," page 123; the description of the Kinburg Regiment on page 124; the speech on war that begins "The army is like a factory…," page 126; the thoughts on "living unconsciously" and "One's work, clothes, furniture, books, one's wife," page 200 — all are taken from Viktor Shklovsky's *A Sentimental Journey: Memoirs, 1917-1922*, translated by Richard Sheldon (Dalkey Archive Press/ Deep Vellum).

The speech by Marusya on page 177 is taken from Peter Arshinov's *History of the Makhnovist Movement*, translated by Lorraine and Fredy Perlman.

The entries from Wiebe's "journal," page 193, are quoted directly from *Troubles and Triumph* by Peter J. Dyck, translated by John P. Dyck.

The lines that begin with "Black night. White snow…," page 200, are taken from Alexander Blok's poem *The Twelve*, translated by Maria Carlson.

The line "a binding of schoolboy calico, in a brownish black," page 46, comes from "The Bookcase" by Osip Mandelstam; and the phrase "sweet the fat earth," page 217, comes from "Black Earth" by Osip Mandelstam, both translations by Clarence Brown.

This is a novel. All inaccuracies are the author's.